The _Fringe_

of _Kindness_

Short Stories by Wolfie Brandt

The _Fringe_

of _Kindness_

Short Stories by Wolfie Brandt

To my dear family, friends and colleagues, far and wide, I offer my sincere gratitude for all your assistance, love and support over many years. W. B.

Contents

A Bag of Oranges   7

The Hand of God   25

Peter Schilling   43

The Girl   45

The Storyteller   61

A Mouse Named Cloud   71

The Playground in the Park   77

The Cup   107

The Castle at Nightfall

      Part 1   The Visitors   121

      Part 2   The Residents   132

      Part 3   The Baroness   142

      Part 4   The Return   153

      Part 5   Epilogue   182

* * * * * * * * * *

A Bag of Oranges

Mrs Prudence Jane Prior – guardian of the neighbourhood, defender of her community's moral code, governess of local affairs, and protector of all who were blessed to reside within the catchment of her own personal monthly news bulletins – sat attentively by the bay window in her front room and looked out upon the street. Her husband sat peacefully in the sunroom at the other end of the house reading an old paperback.

Prudence loved being the secretary of her bowls club, a consultant to the primary school's P & C, and a member of the historical society; but above all she loved being the chair for the local Neighbourhood Watch committee, (especially now that the dashing and handsome Constable Peters had become their latest liaison officer). So, when she had a brief moment to herself – when there was just a small portion of her time when members of the community didn't require her services or her opinion on any matters within the domain of her expertise – she would examine her world from this window and make sure that all remained orderly, calm and well therein.

The window offered her a 180-degree view, and she could see almost two blocks in each direction. This became four blocks when she utilised the Zeiss binoculars she got for Christmas. They were a gift to herself, and had enhanced her observation skills immensely.

Once, at a distance of approximately one hundred metres, she saw a young man and woman sitting in the front seat of some kind of fancy European sports car. They were engaged in the throes of a passionate and tongue-locked embrace. It took a few minutes of close observation to confirm exactly what was occurring, but then she determined a call to Constable Peters was in fact very necessary.

7

On another occasion, she saw a young man walking a black dachshund. He allowed the said canine to defecate in the middle of the nature strip, and then failed to package and remove the offending material, according to section 19, part 3, sub-clause 2 of the Dog Act. Another call to Constable Peters was certainly required.

So, there she sat, calm in the knowledge that on this particular day all seemed very peaceful in the world. It was late morning, the sun was shining, and a light breeze blew a few more petals off her Jacaranda tree. She finally conceded that nothing much else was happening.

She thought another cup of Earl Grey was in order, and was just about to get up when an ambulance arrived outside the home of Kathleen Wright, directly opposite. She pressed her nose against the glass and felt her heart quicken as two fine-looking, male officers alighted from the vehicle, opened the gate and walked up to Kathleen's front door.

"Trevor," Prudence called to her husband, "looks like Kathleen's off to hospital again. Poor thing. It was just last month she went off by ambulance, wasn't it, Trevor?"

There was silence from the far end of the house.

"I must try to call her when she returns . . . but she never answers her phone. I keep on getting her answering machine, and she never calls me back. Maybe I won't bother."

Still, complete silence.

Paramedic officer Stephen Joyce stood casually by the window in the sunroom, sipping a cup of tea and looking out across the back garden. His younger partner was in the next room, assisting Mrs Wright to collect her medications and other belongings.

After twenty-five years in the Ambulance Service, Stephen had responded to the vast majority of clinical situations that nature and misadventure could throw in his direction. So, he was grateful when, on occasions like this, he had a more relaxed and routine case which didn't involve the stress of emergency work. They were simply

8

taking Mrs Wright to hospital for some surgery on her legs, and she would be spending a week or so there while she recuperated.

On occasions like this, Stephen could take his time, chat a little to the patient, and also spend a few moments looking about their home and property. He loved to study real estate, and felt privileged to work in an industry which allowed him so much access to people's homes. Over the years he'd seen it all – from the wealthiest and most opulent of harbour-side mansions to the most squalid and derelict of makeshift shelters. For Stephen, each was unique and interesting in its own special way.

Mrs Wright's home was a well-preserved and very pleasant 1930s bungalow. The back garden was larger than he'd expected and, like the house, was orderly and very well loved. A Colebrookdale table and two chairs stood neatly on the patio just outside the back door, and a small wooden shed and an old Hills hoist stood on the left-hand side. Beyond that, a well-maintained lawn stretched for a good twenty metres to the rear fence.

The garden's most striking feature, however, was a row of four mature and healthy orange trees which stood along the right-hand side. Each tree was laden with plump, juicy oranges, and the ground was sprinkled with several that had already fallen.

Mrs Wright walked slowly back into the room, closely followed by Stephen's partner, officer Ross Whitaker, who was struggling with a very large, very full, and obviously very heavy travel bag.

Stephen turned and smiled. "Are we ready, Mrs Wright?"

"Yes, I think so," she replied. She looked back at Ross. "Do you think so?"

Ross nodded silently, his lips pursed, then put the bag down on the floor with a thud.

"I've just been admiring your garden," Stephen said. "I particularly love your orange trees. Do you do your own gardening?"

"Oh, God no!" said Kathleen. "I used to . . . and my husband too, when he was alive. But these days I haven't got the strength to do

9

any of that. I get a gardener in once a month. He keeps things in good order."

"You must like oranges."

"I don't mind them, but my husband used to love them. He'd eat the lot, he would."

"Well, there are certainly a lot of good ones on those trees."

"Yes, most of them are ripe and ready for picking, but I don't want the gardener round while I'm away. So, I suppose they'll be wasted now." She paused and looked out the window, then turned back to Stephen. "Tell you what, why don't you boys have them? Take as many as you want – they're no good to me. They'll just be rotting on the ground by the time I get back."

Stephen thought for a moment and looked over at Ross, who was frowning and shaking his head slowly.

"Are you sure?" Stephen asked.

"Absolutely! Take them all. You can share them at the station. You boys need to keep up your vitamin C."

"Well, that's very kind of you Mrs Wright. I'm quite a fan of the old orange. We don't have time to collect them now, but we could come back later, closer to knock-off time, if that's okay."

"Sure, that's fine. The side gate's unlocked – just come around. You'd be doing me a favour . . . and please, call me Kathleen."

"Okay then," Stephen said, and he drained the last drops from his tea cup. He stepped briefly into the kitchen, gave the cup a quick rinse and placed it in the sink.

"Now, we're ready to go," he said as he returned to the sunroom. "So, would you like us to get the stretcher and we can wheel you to the ambulance? It'll save your legs from walking all the way to the street."

"No thank you," Kathleen said firmly. "I'm sure that busy-body across the road has been glued to her front window, watching every movement since you turned up. I'll walk out if you don't mind, and I'd like to sit in the front seat too. That way, I'll enjoy the ride."

Stephen took her by the arm and they walked slowly to the front door. Ross followed, silently straining with the bag. On the front porch, Kathleen took a key from her handbag and locked the door, and as she did so she whispered to them both. "Don't make it obvious, but can you look across the road to the house directly opposite and tell me if there's a woman watching us from her front bay window?"

Stephen casually put on his sunglasses, turned slowly towards the street and focused carefully on the house in question. "Hmm," he said softly. "That would be the woman with her face plastered up against the glass, would it?"

"Yes . . . that would be the one," said Kathleen with a sigh.

With all this activity, Prudence was starting to fog up the window, so she pulled an old tissue from her sleeve and wiped the glass. Years of experience had taught her to always have a spare tissue ready for occasions like these.

"Oh, Trevor," she called out, "they're making their way to the ambulance now! They're just coming down the front path. Poor old thing – I can see she's limping a bit, but she's such a stoic. That fine officer is supporting her, I can tell. Wonder if he does first-aid lectures. I might make an enquiry and see if he'll come around to the club. My goodness, she must be going for a while. That other officer with the bag looks like he's going to get a hernia."

Ross just managed to get the bag into the rear of the ambulance, while Stephen and Kathleen made their way to the front passenger door.

"Oh, she is courageous!" Prudence continued. "She's getting up into the front seat. That officer's giving her a bit of a lift. That must be fun. I'll have to try that, if ever I get sick."

Stephen assisted Kathleen with her seat belt and then jumped into the back of the ambulance. He noted that since leaving the front porch, Kathleen hadn't said a word. Even now she sat tight-lipped and motionless, staring directly down the road. It was obvious she

11

wished to minimise any elements of drama that this departing spectacle may provide to her inquisitive neighbour. Ross started the engine, looked back to check that Stephen was seated, and then drove off slowly.

For her part, Prudence fully utilized every technical feature of her Zeiss binoculars until the ambulance completely disappeared from sight.

When they were well away from the house, Kathleen suddenly took a deep breath, looked about in all directions with a broad smile and declared, "Ahhh! It's so nice to get out of the house on such a sunny day. Thankyou boys, you've been marvellous."

Ross nodded and continued to focus on the road ahead. Stephen couldn't help himself and piped-up from the back. "So, I'm guessing you don't have the best relationship with the lady across the road."

"Yes, that's right," said Kathleen. "She's quite a stickybeak. Way too involved in other people's affairs, I'm afraid. She keeps on wanting me to join clubs and committees and things like that. At this stage of my life, I'd rather be left alone."

"Yes, of course . . . that sounds fair," Stephen said, and he thought he'd better change the subject.

So, over the next twenty minutes, Kathleen and Stephen chatted about everything else, and told lots of jokes, while Ross listened attentively in professional silence. At one stage, when Kathleen told a yarn that could only be described as 'surprisingly wicked' for someone her age, Ross finally gave in and began to laugh. He kept on chuckling all the way to the hospital, until he remembered the luggage. Stephen told his partner not to stress, and he went off to find two wheelchairs. They then delivered Kathleen and her bag safely to the ward.

"Now, you boys make sure you collect all those oranges," Kathleen reminded them. "I don't want to see a single orange on my lawn when I return. Are we clear? And when I get back, you make sure you pop in sometime for another cup of tea."

Stephen smiled. "And maybe a scone?"

12

"Yes," said Kathleen. "And a scone."

Ross glanced from Kathleen back to his partner, then looked out the window and shook his head slowly.

The remainder of their shift proved to be very busy, and neither Stephen nor his partner had time to think about Kathleen and her generous offer. On the following day, however, there was little work, and by late afternoon they were sitting in their favourite cafe for the second time. The conversation had run dry, and Stephen took another sip from his cappuccino and stared out the window.

"So, when we've finished these coffees, we'll go off and get those oranges," he suddenly announced.

Ross's jaw dropped. "You're not serious. I thought you were joking about that."

"No, not at all. I'd never joke about fresh oranges. It's a win-win situation, isn't it? She gets the oranges taken away and not rotting on her lawn, and we get a load of fresh fruit at the station. Sounds like a great deal to me."

"Why didn't we get them earlier? We've had plenty of down-time today."

"Well, think about it," Stephen said. "We can't risk having all those oranges in the back of the ambulance and then getting an emergency job, can we? We've got to collect them close to finishing time, so we're guaranteed to get them back to the station."

"I suppose so," Ross conceded, with a small sigh. "But I've got to say, I feel a bit uncomfortable about this."

"Hey, don't sweat about it – it's perfectly legal. She's simply giving us a gift we can share at the station." Stephen glanced at his watch. "Now, I think the time's about right, so finish up and let's get going."

The arrival of the ambulance outside Kathleen's house did not escape the attention of Prudence, who seemed to have a sixth sense regarding any movements within the street.

13

"Oh, Trevor," she called, as she stared out her front window. "Looks like Kathleen's returning from hospital. The ambulance has just pulled up. That was very quick – especially when you consider the bag she took. It was just yesterday morning she left, wasn't it?"

She moved right up to the window and focused carefully on the ambulance as both Stephen and Ross alighted from the front of the vehicle. "Hmm; she doesn't seem to be sitting in the front seat. She must be on the stretcher in the back, poor thing."

The officers made their way through the front gate, then cut across the lawn and walked down the side path of the residence.

"That's rather strange. They're not taking her out of the ambulance. Those two officers have just gone around the back. Something's going on, Trevor, I can tell. Something's not quite right."

Stephen and Ross walked to the middle of the garden and surveyed the neat row of orange trees and their fully ripened produce. Each tree stood about three metres high, was well-rounded in shape and emblazoned in bright orange. Stephen noted that even more oranges had now fallen on the lawn.

"Well, what do we do now?" Ross asked, with a tone of underlying impatience.

"Start collecting oranges of course," Stephen said. "Haven't you ever picked fruit before? First, we've got to shake these trees. Just hold on to a strong branch and give it a good shake. You'll find most of the oranges will fall off. Look . . . like this." He moved forward and gave one of the trees a firm shake. Just as he had predicted, a large number of oranges fell immediately, producing a rapid succession of dull thuds as they struck the soft grass and began rolling about in different directions. As they fell, three or four of them hit him on the head.

"Hmm, so that's how you do it," said Ross, trying to suppress a smile. Then he looked up at the tree. "Well, what about those ones up there?" He pointed to a few oranges that remained attached to the

14

upper branches, well out of reach. "I'm not climbing any trees today."

"Oh, don't worry about those ones. We'll have plenty with all the ones on the ground. Now, let's get on with it."

"Hold on a second," said Ross. "How are we going to *carry* them all? By the time we shake all these trees we'll have loads. I'm not taking them round to the ambulance by hand. You didn't think about how we'd carry them, did you?"

"That's a good point," Stephen noted calmly.

"Why don't we just find a bucket and take a dozen or so. That'd be enough for the station."

"No, these oranges are superb. I'm not letting them go to waste. Besides, we're helping our friend Kathleen, remember. She said she didn't want to see any rotting on the lawn."

"Well you come up with an idea," Ross demanded. "We're going to need a bloody big container to hold this lot."

Stephen stood deep in thought and didn't say a word. He started to tap his fingers on his lips and slowly looked about the garden for several seconds. "Okay," he said suddenly, "I've got an idea."

Prudence was becoming increasingly frustrated by the inability of her Zeiss binoculars to penetrate through Kathleen's house and provide a view to the back garden. Something was happening back there and she just had to know what it was. Kathleen obviously wasn't in the ambulance, so what were those officers doing while she was still in hospital? Though her curiosity was overwhelming, she wasn't about to leave the comfort and security of her lounge room. She focused her high-powered lenses on both of the windows at the front of the house, and although there didn't seem to be any movement within, the shadiness of those rooms precluded a clear view.

She remembered a Reader's Digest survey which concluded that the ambulance paramedics have the most trusted profession. Now, however, she was starting to question that notion. These two officers were bold and brazen, and obviously up to no good! Her hands had become quite sweaty as she firmly grasped the binoculars and closely scrutinized the edges of Kathleen's property for any hint of activity.

She was just starting to feel that a phone call to Constable Peters was in order, when Ross came briskly along the side path and returned to the ambulance. He opened the rear door and pulled out the stretcher, its legs and wheels dropping into position so it stood upright on the street. He then rummaged in the back of the ambulance and located a large, crimson package which he unceremoniously threw down upon the stretcher. With a stern look of dissatisfaction, he pushed the stretcher into the property and down the side path.

"Oh Trevor, they're getting the stretcher!" Prudence shouted. "My goodness; Kathleen must be at home after all. It's rather surprising I didn't see her return." She averted her eyes from the street for a moment, deep in thought. "Oh, I know! She must have come home sometime last night while we were sleeping. Those ambulance officers do that sort of thing you know – bring people home very quietly in the middle of the night. But now they're collecting her again. She obviously came home too soon. She must be ailing, poor thing. Really, I don't know why those doctors send someone home when they're not fully recuperated!"

While Ross was at the ambulance, Stephen had been hard at work. He'd fully shaken the remaining trees and was more than satisfied with the abundance of oranges that had fallen to the ground. Then he'd found a rake in the garden shed, and by the time Ross returned with the stretcher, had managed to rake most of the oranges into a large pile.

"Did you find it?" Stephen asked.

"Yes . . . yes . . . I've got it," Ross replied, with a long, drawn-out sigh.

"Good; then lay it out here." Stephen pointed to the grass immediately alongside the heap of oranges.

Ross unfolded the large crimson bag and spread it out upon the ground. He then unzipped it along its entire length and opened it fully. They both looked down upon the bag, its wide mouth gaping open in readiness.

"I can't believe we're using this," said Ross, shaking his head a little.

"But it's perfect," said Stephen. "Look at it – just like it was made for the job."

"Yeah, but it wasn't made for *this* job, was it. I have to say, this is not exactly by the book."

"Oh, don't stress. So, the load's a bit fresher than usual . . . and we get to keep the bag."

"I don't think I can eat an orange after it's been in there," Ross exclaimed stiffly.

"Don't be silly. It's just a vinyl bag, and it's never been used. Now let's get on with it."

They both knelt down and began tossing oranges into the bag. After a minute or two, it started to get quite full, so Ross held it open to maximise the volume while Stephen continued to throw the remaining oranges into every section. As he did so, he came across one particular orange that, due to the randomness of nature, had grown considerably larger than the rest.

"Oh, look at this juicy specimen," Stephen said with a grin. "I'm keeping this one for myself." He put the enormous orange to one side while he finished filling, and then placed it carefully on the very top of the load before zipping up the bag completely.

"Okay, I think that should do it," he said with an air of pride. "Now, let's put it on the stretcher and get out of here."

They both took a firm hold of the straps at each end of the heavily laden bag, and then with all their strength lifted it up onto the waiting stretcher.

"Bloody hell!" shouted Ross, as the bag thumped down. "This thing weighs at ton!"

17

"Oh, stop whinging. It's nothing the stretcher can't handle. Start pushing."

As they made their way round the side of the house and hauled the stretcher onto the front lawn, Prudence was on to them like a fly on a jam tart.

"Oh, my goodness, Trevor, look at this!" she cried, tightly clutching her binoculars. "Kathleen's passed away! This is simply inexcusable! They've sent her home from the hospital, obviously in such feeble condition that the poor old dear has gone and expired!" She felt her pulse quicken as she sniffed the distant scent of controversy. "I'll be taking this up with the Minister for Health, I can assure you. This is indefensible!"

The front lawn was a little uneven, and the large weight on the stretcher made it bear down heavily into the soft grass. Both front wheels got stuck in a small furrow, and despite a great deal of pushing and shaking by the officers, the stretcher would not advance.

"Those ambulance men are a bit rough!" Prudence noted anxiously. "The poor old girl's just passed on and these blokes are shaking her about like a jelly on a roller-coaster. A little more respect for the departed may be in order."

Both Stephen and Ross took hold of the front of the stretcher and heaved it upwards to free the wheels. As they did so, the load of oranges shifted and tumbled in a small stampede to the lower end of the bag, which bulged outwards and toppled off the side of the stretcher.

"Oh, Trevor, this is disgraceful! Haven't these ambulance men acquired any skills with regard to the appropriate handling of deceased persons? You can't toss a body about like this. I'll be making a complaint Trevor. And I'll be telling the members of the bowls club not to get sick while these fellows are around . . . and certainly not to die! This is very unsatisfactory treatment."

Back on Kathleen's front lawn, Ross was starting to fume. "Oh, for God's sake! I told you we had too many oranges," he shouted.

18

"Hey, show a bit of backbone will you," Stephen replied, as he pushed the empty stretcher onto the front path. "Now, let's just pick it up again and wheel it out of here."

With one more heave they lifted the bag and slammed it down on the stretcher. Then they pushed it out the front gate and onto the street behind the ambulance. Just as Stephen was opening the rear doors, his portable radio sparked into action.

"Car 6-5-8," the radio controller announced. "Sorry guys, I know it's close to finishing time, but you're the nearest car to this job. I've got a cardiac patient with breathing difficulties just a few blocks from you."

"Bugger!" Stephen shouted. "I don't believe it! Hardly done a bloody thing all day, and right now of all times, we get something serious!"

"Oh, what a shame," Ross said calmly with a wry smile. "Looks like we'll have to leave all these oranges after all. So, Stephen, what would you like me to do now?"

Stephen glared at his partner for a moment. "You go to the car radio and accept the job before the controller calls us again," he said tersely. "Then come back here. We're going to have to ditch this bag."

Ross did as instructed and headed off to the front of the ambulance.

Stephen stared at the bag of oranges laid out before him and took a deep, calming breath. "Oh well," he thought to himself. "We can leave the oranges here and maybe come back for them later. But I'm not leaving that big one. I'm going to take that one now and eat it at the hospital." He unzipped the bag a little and took a close peek inside.

"Oh, Trevor, what are they up to now!" Prudence exclaimed. "As if they haven't done enough to the old girl. This is undignified! There'll definitely be a mention of this in my next news bulletin."

"Where's that big orange?" Stephen whispered to himself, as he carefully scanned inside the bag. "I know I put you on top. Where did you roll to? Ah, there you are! Right down the end of course." He reached deep into the bag and fished about at the far end till he felt his prized orange.

"Oh, my God!! This is outrageous!" Prudence shouted, and she turned from the window and headed for her telephone. "What sort of fellows do they accept in the ambulance service these days? That's it! I've had enough! I'm calling Constable Peters."

Her fingers followed a well-worn path on the face of her telephone, as she rapidly pressed the number that was deeply embedded in her memory. A young woman's voice answered the call.

"Wattle Bay Police – this is Constable Witherspoon. How may I help you?"

"Ah, Constable Witherspoon, this is Prudence Prior from the Neighbourhood Watch. May I please speak to Constable Peters? It's rather urgent."

There was a muffling of the phone, but Prudence could just make out the young woman's voice in the distance. "Hey, Sarge. It's a lady from Neighbourhood Watch. She wants to speak to Peters – says it's urgent. Is he in?"

After a moment a mature man's voice came on the line.

"Hello, this is Senior Sergeant Bob Stanhope. I'm afraid Constable Peters is not available. Can I help you?"

"Ah yes, Sergeant, that's good," replied Prudence. "I'm sure you can help. There are two ambulance officers carting a dead body out of a house opposite where I live, and they're shaking it about and then throwing it on the ground, and being thoroughly disrespectful. And now one of the officers is – I'm almost too ashamed to say it – but one of the officers is fondling the body in the middle of the street!"

There were several seconds of complete silence from the other end of the phone.

"Sergeant, are you there?"

"Excuse me, but who exactly is this?" the Sergeant asked.

20

"Prudence Prior – Neighbourhood Watch."

There were a few more seconds of silence.

"Is this the same Prudence Prior that has rung up Constable Peters several times in the last few months?"

"Well, yes, there's been a lot of criminal behaviour occurring lately and . . ."

"Criminal behaviour! Didn't you ring up and say that two people were having unrestrained sex in the street, in clear view of the local residents, and when we came around we found a young, innocent couple having a snog in an Alfa Romeo?"

"Yes . . . but it was getting quite heated and . . ."

"And then, didn't you ring up another time and tell us that a savage dog was destroying property and terrorising the neighbourhood, and when we sent a car round they found that a small dachshund had dropped a minute bowel motion on the nature strip?"

"Ah, yes, that was me too . . . but according to the Dog Act . . ."

"And now you're telling us that two ambulance officers – *paramedics* I presume – our most trusted colleagues, are not only dragging a dead body out of a house and throwing it about, but they're also groping it in the middle of the street. Is that right?"

"Well . . . yes! I know it's incredible, but that's what it looks like to me! I can see them quite clearly with my binoculars."

"Binoculars! Mrs Prior, I'm not listening to any more of this nonsense, and I'm certainly not sending a car round this time. If there is an ambulance crew in your street, I'm sure they're doing a wonderfully professional job and upholding the highest standards of conduct as expected from all members of their service."

"But Sergeant, I'm a trusted member of the community, and this report is thoroughly accurate, I can assure you."

"And you say you're talking about ambulance officers in full uniform, with a *real* ambulance – yes?"

"Absolutely!"

"So, tell me, what are they doing right now?"

21

Prudence moved back to the window, clutching the phone in one hand and her binoculars in the other. She focused carefully on the street outside. Stephen and Ross had lifted the bag from the stretcher and hauled it back to the footpath by Kathleen's front fence. Together, in unison, they swung the bag a few times and then launched it high over the fence, so it landed behind a couple of small bushes in the garden. Then they ran back to the ambulance and sped off down the street.

Prudence yelled into the phone. "Oh, my God! They've just thrown the body into the front garden and now they're making a getaway!"

"Mrs Prior, are you at home alone?" the Sergeant asked calmly.

"Well, no, not exactly. My husband's here too."

"And, your husband, is he a sensible man?"

"Yes, I believe so."

"So, what does he think of all this?"

"Oh, he hasn't seen anything. He never sees anything."

"Ah-haaa!! I want you to get your husband and ask him to do you a favour."

"What's that?"

"Ask him to take you to the doctor. I think you need a complete review of your medications."

"But Sergeant . . ."

"Mrs Prior, that's enough!! If you phone again with this sort of rubbish, I'll have you charged with public mischief! Goodbye!" The sergeant slammed down the phone and the line went dead.

Prudence sat down by the window and quietly stared into the empty street. Her shoulders slumped and the phone fell from her hand onto the floor. She remained perfectly still, her face expressionless, her binoculars sitting in her lap. Outside, she could see that the sun had just set, and the bright colours of the street were slowly surrendering to a light veil of drab grey.

A thin, elderly gentleman wearing a dressing gown and thick reading glasses walked slowly into the room. He placed a paperback novel and an empty whiskey glass down on a side table, and then looked over at his wife.

"Prudence, are you alright?" Trevor asked, as he carefully removed two ear plugs from his ears.

Prudence made no response. She sat motionless and continued to stare out the window in complete silence. Trevor walked over and studied her closely.

"Prudence?"

There was still no response.

He picked up the telephone from the floor, gave a large sigh and slowly dialled a number.

"Hello. It's Trevor Prior here. Yes . . . my wife seems to be having a turn. I'd like you to send an ambulance please."

* * * * * * * * * * *

The Hand of God

Most calls in the life of a paramedic are easily forgotten. Things like abdominal pain, faints, minor injuries, seizures, and the myriad of respiratory and cardiac disorders, become routine and are quickly lost from memory. Experience is gained, but the particulars of the case are easily dismissed and the slate is wiped clean. Sometimes, when Stephen got to the end of a shift, he couldn't even remember what cases he'd done that day.

Yet, there are some calls in the life of a paramedic that are never forgotten. Some unique and extraordinary cases become ingrained in the memory of the officer, to be recalled repeatedly throughout the years, sometimes during social engagements and sometimes in moments of solitude.

That's the nature of ambulance work. It can become very routine, yet, remains quite unpredictable.

* * * * * * * * * * *

The morning had been fairly normal. Stephen and Ross had attended to a chest infection in a nursing home, a faint at the Soldiers Club, and a distressed young woman with neck pain and a damaged BMW.

By 1300, they had arrived back at the ambulance station and were keen to have a small lunch break. Stephen had bought a large container of chicken pasta from his favourite take-away, and had just placed it down on the meal room table when the phone rang.

25

"I'm sorry guys," the controller said on the line. "I know you've just got back, but I've got someone hit by a train at Rivendell Station."

"Any more information?" Stephen asked.

"No, that's it for the moment."

"Okay, got it."

Stephen put the phone down, picked up his pasta and headed for the door. He felt hungry, had a slight headache, and jobs of this nature always produced some tension in his stomach. As he passed the toilet door in the corridor, he gave a few small knocks and called to his partner. "Ross, we've got a job. Someone hit by a train at Rivendell."

"Oh, crap!" came the resonating reply from within the small, tiled room.

In the ambulance, Stephen confirmed the details over the radio and was reaching for his vest when Ross quickly entered the plant room. "Have we got back-up?" he asked, as he jumped into the driver's seat.

"Yeah, there's a second car coming from Forest Hill, and a rescue truck and manager from the city. But we're going to get there first."

The drive to the Rivendell railway station took about four minutes. Amidst the flash of beacons and the wail of the sirens, Ross wove a path through the heavy traffic of the commercial district. Within the muffled cabin, Stephen carefully put on his gloves and thought about the scene. Being one of the larger suburban stations, it was often busy, but at this time, not as busy as the peak periods of the morning and evening. It was also completely above ground, so he felt grateful the weather was fine.

As they approached the scene, they received further information over the radio. The controller said there had been several calls but the details were still vague. There was apparently a woman, and most of the calls indicated she had died.

They parked the ambulance near the base of a large flight of stairs that led up to a pedestrian concourse above the station. A short distance away, an empty highway patrol car with its hazard lights on was parked awkwardly by the side of the road. Another police van with two more officers was also pulling up as Stephen and Ross got out of the ambulance. They grabbed their equipment and headed for the stairs.

As they went up, Stephen noted a middle-aged woman who was slowly making her way down. She was sobbing uncontrollably and trying to wipe the tears from her face. One of the police officers went to her and took out his notebook, while the other ran ahead.

Stephen and Ross entered the concourse, which ran above and transversely to the platforms at the northern end of the station. They were met by the stationmaster who hurried over to them. A short, somewhat rotund man with a southern European background, Stephen had met him once before, when just two weeks earlier he had attended to a diabetic on platform four. On that occasion the stationmaster had been calm with a very cheery disposition. Today, however, he seemed very stressed. He was struggling to get his words out between deep breaths, his face was flushed, and tiny beads of sweat covered his forehead.

"Thank you, thank you for coming," he said anxiously. "Quickly, this way, down on platform one. Quickly please!"

"Okay, but just tell me what's happening," Stephen demanded, as both he and Ross paced across the concourse. "We've been told there's a woman. Is she dead?"

"Oh yes, she's dead . . . she's very dead."

"Well, did she throw herself under the train or was it an accident?"

"The people on the platform are saying she jumped. All of a sudden, she just jumped in front of the train . . . but she was carrying a child – a little boy. It's just terrible! Come quickly please; I need you to see! I've got a lot of upset people down there."

27

"She was carrying a child!" Stephen shouted, and he glanced at Ross striding beside him. "Is the child dead too?"

"I don't know, I just don't know. That's why I need you to come and see!"

Stephen's heart was already racing after carrying the gear up from the road, but now he felt some palpitations in his neck and instinctively took several deep breaths. They made their way through a small group of people that had gathered at the top of the stairs to platforms one and two.

"Out of the way please . . . please move!" shouted the stationmaster, and they all silently stepped to one side.

As they descended the stairs, Stephen could see the platforms stretched out before him. They were bathed in sunlight but unusually empty, having already been cleared by the staff. About fifty metres away, out on the platform near a small guard's office and waiting room, Stephen noted a solitary railway guard who stood facing them.

At the base of the stairs, alongside platform one, stood the tail end of a large passenger train. It was evident that the train driver must have had difficulty stopping because only the final two carriages stood against the platform. The rest of the train extended out behind the stairs, below the pedestrian concourse and past the end of the station. Several passengers were leaving the last two carriages, and a police officer and some railway staff were directing them to the stairs.

On the other side of the platform, a highway patrol officer had gathered a small number of witnesses. Among them, Stephen could see a young man and woman embracing each other, and an elderly man who stood stern-faced, just staring at the ground. As Stephen and Ross followed the stationmaster onto the platform, the highway patrol officer came running over to them. "These people are saying she was carrying a small boy, but I've only seen the woman on the tracks," he said.

"Yes, I know about the child," the stationmaster replied abruptly. "I'm taking the paramedics there now."

Stephen called back to the officer as they continued along the platform. "You deal with those people there, and we'll call you if we need you, okay." The officer nodded and headed back to his witnesses.

Stephen could hear the sound of sirens in the distance but was not sure if it was one of the backup crews or more police.

They soon approached the railway guard who stood alone near the entrance to the waiting room. Late middle-aged with a grey beard, he said nothing, but continued to gaze solemnly down the platform towards the stairs.

A large awning sheltered that section of the platform. It cast a deep shadow across the tracks, and as Stephen and Ross's eyes adjusted to the light, they became aware of the woman. Her bloodied and torn remains were mixed with shredded clothing and strewn across five or six metres of the track. Some pieces lay between the rails and some were scattered outside. It was clear she had aligned herself with the full brunt of the train as it came into the station. The top part of her torso – the head, upper chest and one arm – was recognisable as it lay face down by the rails. Most of the rest was so fragmented it could hardly be identified.

In that brief moment Stephen had seen enough, and he turned his eyes away. "So, where's the boy?" he asked the stationmaster.

"He's down there I think," the stationmaster said breathlessly, pointing to the tracks a little further down the line. "But I'm sorry, I'm not going any further. I just can't see any more!"

Stephen put down his equipment and leaned out over the edge of the platform, focusing carefully on the railway tracks. At first, he saw nothing of interest – just a few old drink cans, wrappers and odd pieces of rubbish. But then he noticed what appeared to be a small pile of dark rags or clothing about ten metres away. It lay motionless on the outside of the track, immediately under the overhanging edge of the platform. As he continued to stare closely into the shadows, he could just make out the shape of a small hand protruding from the material.

29

Stephen turned back to Ross. "Get on the radio and tell them to keep everyone coming. We've got one deceased and one young child. I'm not sure if the child is dead or seriously injured, but we'll give another report as soon as possible. Oh, and tell the other crew to bring down at least four or five sheets. We've got to cover that before anyone else sees it."

Ross unclipped his portable radio and moved a few metres away over the platform.

"How do I get down there?" Stephen asked the stationmaster. "Do I have to jump?"

"Yes, it's the only way down."

"And the track's safe, of course."

"Yes, absolutely. Everything is diverted through platforms three and four."

Stephen squatted at the very edge of the platform, and then jumped down onto the ballast stones by the side of the tracks. The large stones were uneven and his landing was a little unsteady, but he managed to keep on his feet. He began to walk toward the small boy who still lay silent and motionless by the base of the platform. As he got closer, he could see that the boy was lying on his side, huddled in a tight ball with his knees pressed up against his chest. He wore a matching, dark denim jacket and trousers which were covered by a fine layer of grimy railway dust. His head lay supported by the crook of his left arm, while his other arm was stretched out towards the tracks. His face remained hidden by the sleeve of his jacket and a large, dirty mop of black, wavy hair. Apart from his hands and a small pair of red shoes, the little bundle of a child, all wrapped up in dark clothing, seemed to be consumed by the shadows and ballast beneath the edge of the platform.

Stephen crouched down beside the boy. He could just perceive the slightest movement of his jacket as the tiny child took a breath; and then another. Stephen gently placed his hand on the boy's outstretched arm, and as he did so, the boy slowly raised his head and looked up at him. His face was covered in railway dust, just like his

30

clothing, and he appeared quite bewildered, gazing at Stephen without saying a word.

Stephen's first response was relief, since the boy was awake and seemed to be fine. But then Stephen felt a heaviness in his heart. He guessed the boy could only be about three or four years old. His face was so sweet, and his large hazel eyes continued to stare back at him with an innocence that could hardly be defined.

"Hey, little fella," Stephen said softly. "Are you alright?"

The boy made no reply but suddenly pushed himself up into a sitting position. He gave a slow, deep yawn, then turned his head to one side and looked out vaguely across the tracks. It was like he had just woken from a long sleep, and Stephen felt he couldn't comprehend where he was or what had happened.

"Is he okay?" called a voice from above. Stephen looked up and saw Ross leaning out over the platform. Next to him was the stationmaster, peering down anxiously.

"I think so. I can't believe it," Stephen said.

"Oh, thank God," said the stationmaster, with a crackle in his voice.

Stephen ran his gloved hands around the boy's head, checking for any blood that may be hidden in his thick, black hair. Then he checked his neck, his back, his legs and arms. He unbuttoned his jacket and carefully felt his chest and tummy. It all seemed intact – there was no blood, no deformity, no calling out in pain. All the while, the little boy sat there calmly without saying a word, just staring at the railway tracks beside him.

Stephen had kept himself crouched down beside the boy, shielding him from any view of his mother. Now he turned back briefly and glanced at her remains. Then he looked up and across the platform. He could see that the second crew had arrived and were heading towards them carrying some equipment and several sheets. He called out to Ross again. "You can call off the rescue team. I'm going to pick him up and give him to you; but I'm not going to do it till the tracks are covered. You understand?"

31

Ross nodded and ran down the platform to direct the second crew to cover the body.

"Do you need me anymore?" asked the stationmaster. "It's just that I've got a lot of things I have to attend to."

"No, we're fine," Stephen said. "My partner and I can manage from now, thank you."

The stationmaster headed off hastily and started talking on his radio. A moment later, Ross came back and knelt down on the platform. "It's done," he said.

Stephen whispered to the boy. "Okay, my little man – let's get out of here." He carefully picked up the child and held him in his arms for a few seconds. Still the boy said nothing, but seemed slightly anxious and began to breathe a little faster. Stephen passed him up to Ross, who stood up slowly and cradled him while Stephen climbed back onto the platform.

"He looks fine," Ross whispered, with an air of disbelief.

"I know – it's incredible," Stephen said. "But we're going to have to check him more closely, and I don't want to do it here. Let's go over the other side of the platform and back up to the main office." He glanced down the tracks towards the mother's remains. He could see the second crew had done a tidy job with the sheets, and were now climbing back onto the platform.

"Here, you take him," Ross said, holding out the boy. "I think he wants you. He's getting a bit restless." The boy held out his arms to Stephen, who took him and gave him a gentle hug. Now he seemed more alert and was staring intently down the platform toward the stairs.

"Hey, it's okay. Everything's going to be alright," Stephen said softly in his ear.

The boy peered over Stephen's shoulder and continued to focus on the platform. He was slowly becoming aware of his surroundings, and something uneasy was stirring in his memory. As it did so, his sense of bewilderment was gradually turning to fear. The station steps, the platform, the train coming in – now he knew where he was, and suddenly the boy found his voice.

"Mummy!" he called out in a painfully small and sharp cry. "I want my mummy." He looked about rapidly in all directions. "Where's my mummy?" he cried again, and his eyes filled with tears.

There are some questions you wish you'd never been asked. Over the years, Stephen had seen his fair share of trauma. For the most part, he had learned to accept and manage it. It had become technical. If the patient wasn't dead, they could be postured, ventilated, cannulated. Most of the time blood pressure could be maintained. Injuries could be splinted and bandaged. The mechanics of his profession had become automatic and somewhat emotionless.

But this situation was different. How was he to bandage the suffering of a small, innocent child? How does one splint a broken heart? How do you repair the loss of a mother's love? It was moments like these that Stephen found the most difficult to manage. He could only imagine what sort of mental torment was felt by a woman, who would not only throw herself in front of a train, but who also believed it better to take her child with her. He was struggling for words, but felt he had to say something to the boy. He glanced at Ross who was pressing his lips tight and shaking his head slowly.

"Mummy's not here at the moment. But we're here, and we're going to keep you safe." It was all that Stephen could think of, and he wasn't prepared to say any more. The boy continued to cry and he grasped Stephen's neck firmly with his arms.

The second crew was back on the platform and they quickly came over. There was an older female officer called Grace, who Stephen knew quite well, and a younger man he had not met before. Stephen recalled that Grace had children of her own.

"Do you need us?" Grace asked, as she studied the crying boy. "Do you want me to hold him?"

"No, I think I'm okay," Stephen replied. "You could go back to the police officer who's dealing with the witnesses. Some of them may need your help. And you can help Ross carry some of our gear."

Grace's young partner seemed a little excited. Stephen guessed that he hadn't been in the service long, and this was most likely his first railway job.

"Was the boy . . .?" he started to ask, with a look of astonishment.

"Yes, yes," Stephen said, quickly interrupting him, "but let's not talk about it now. I just want to get him off the platform. We're going to take him up to the stationmaster's office before we head to the hospital, so if you see the manager, could you tell him we're there."

"Sure," Grace replied, and they started to collect the equipment on the platform.

Stephen and Ross took the boy around the far end of the waiting room and along the other side of the platform. They could see that more police and railway personnel were arriving at the scene. Leaving Grace and her partner with the police and witnesses, they made their way back up the stairs to the main office. The boy had been resting his head on Stephen's shoulder and crying a little, but was just starting to settle as they knocked on the office door.

The stationmaster opened the door while talking on the phone, and he gestured for them to come inside. They made their way into the large office and waited patiently for a few moments while he finished his call.

". . . So, I need you here immediately," he said, somewhat tensely. "I've got to get this line open within the hour." He hung up the phone, and then turned to face Stephen.

"Do you mind if we do another quick check on him in here?" Stephen asked. "I just wanted to get him off the platform to somewhere more private."

"No, of course," said the stationmaster. "You do anything you want – please, take your time. Do you need a chair?" He quickly moved his chair towards them.

"Thank you, that's fine," Stephen said, and he gently sat the boy down and knelt beside him. Stephen was pleased that he had stopped crying and was now completely calm. "Hey, little fella, what's your name?" he asked.

"Peter," the boy replied, with a sweet, little voice.

"Well, Peter, do you know who we are?"

The boy hesitated for a moment. "A policeman?"

"No . . . not quite. We're ambulance – you understand?"

The boy stared at Stephen. "Yes . . . ambulance."

"Peter, I think you must be a very strong boy, but I just need to take off some of your clothes and check you're okay. Would you let me do that?"

Peter nodded and looked around the room. "Ambulance," he said again.

Stephen carefully took off his denim jacket and pants, and unbuttoned his tiny shirt. Then, while he sat there quietly, Stephen and Ross checked him again thoroughly.

When they finished and were starting to redress him, the stationmaster asked, "So, will you be taking him to the hospital?"

"Yes," Stephen said. "Even though I can't find a mark on him, we do need to take him. I know it's hard to believe, but he seems perfect – as if nothing happened. But he'll have to be checked again by the doctors and kept under observation. And there'll be some follow-up with the police of course, as they look for his family."

Peter had been waiting so patiently, but again he spoke up. "Is my mummy coming *now*?"

Stephen took a deep breath. "Mummy can't come now," he said softly. "Is there someone else living at home with you?"

Peter looked down at the floor, and his face saddened. "Daddy went away."

Stephen shook his head slowly and looked up at his partner. Now, he just didn't know what to say. Both he and Ross heard a small sniff coming from the other side of the room. They turned around and saw a young woman sitting behind a desk in the far corner. She was in her mid-thirties, dressed in a railway uniform, and had been sitting there all along without saying a word. They could see her eyes were quite red, as she had obviously been crying. She now seemed a little embarrassed that she'd been noticed, and she held her hand up to her mouth, looked away, and took a deep, trembling breath.

The stationmaster quickly walked across the room and stood beside her. He placed his hand on her shoulder and gave her a small hug. "This is my good friend Karen," he announced. "She's the train driver."

The train had been cold and insensitive to the plight of the woman and her child. It had acted with precision, and had followed its designated path exactly as directed. It worked without reasoning, without questioning, and it remained both deaf and blind to the world around it.

This was not the case for its driver. Over the past five years, Karen had driven her train countless thousands of kilometres without any form of mishap. She was very content in her role, and proud of her good record. However, she had been told by her work colleagues that the day would come. It was, they said, 'inevitable' if you stay in the job long enough. But as she approached Rivendell at precisely 1301, the possibility of a fatality was the furthest thing from her mind.

As the train glided towards the station, she had maintained good speed and didn't slow. The timetable had this run marked 'express', and she was to pass through Rivendell without stopping. From within her compartment, she could just hear the end of a loud and familiar public-address announcement on the platform.

". . . is a through train and will not stop. Please stand clear."

The few people waiting on the platform were of little interest to her. She had observed this scene so many times before, and there was nothing unusual about it. They were all sitting or standing behind the yellow line. They all had the same disinterested look upon their faces as they casually watched the train approach.

But then, as she drew near to the waiting room, there was suddenly a strange and unexpected movement. A woman walked rapidly towards the edge of the platform while clutching a small child to her chest. The woman remained expressionless, keeping her focus directly ahead, and without hesitation or even the slightest glance at the train or its driver, she leapt in front of the train.

It all happened within a few seconds. Karen had just enough time to scream out the word "NO!!" before the woman and her child disappeared agonisingly below her window frame. From on her driver's seat, Karen was quite conditioned to the feeling of the tracks below, but at that moment, she felt nothing on the rails. She heard only the sound of her own voice screaming as the weight and momentum of the train dragged her disturbingly further down the line.

She had only a vague recollection of the ten minutes immediately following the incident. It remained like a distant memory. She recalled that she tried to stop the train as smoothly as possible, but under the circumstances, it was necessary to overshoot the platform. Then she had gathered her thoughts and made some kind of announcement over the train's public-address system, but now she could hardly remember what she said. After that, she had walked rapidly through the length of the train, spoke briefly to the guard, and met her friend Tony, the stationmaster, on the platform.

Tony had been at the ticket office when he heard someone shouting from the platform below. He went down to investigate, and when a witness told him of the woman's suicide, he had inspected the tracks in a state of shock and disbelief. He made the initial call to the police and ambulance, then ran back to meet Karen and the guard as they came from the train. When Karen told him frantically that the woman had a child, he left her and the guard to assist the passengers, and headed back to inspect the line once more.

37

Everyone in the office could feel Karen's distress. Even little Peter, but he didn't understand. Stephen felt somewhat disappointed that he hadn't considered the driver until now. "Stay with the boy for a second," he said to Ross, and he got up and walked across the room.

"Do you think you're going to be okay?" he asked Karen.

She took another deep breath and nodded. "Yeah, I'll be right."

"I've contacted my regional manager," Tony said, "and we've arranged for Karen to see our counsellor. It's mandatory these days."

"That's good; but when will that be?" Stephen asked.

"I'm waiting for a call, but it should be this afternoon or maybe tomorrow morning."

Stephen looked at Karen again. "If you want, we can take you down to the hospital and you can speak to someone now. They have specialists who can help you with this. I'm taking the boy, and you're welcome to come with us."

Karen thought for a few seconds. "No . . . I'll be alright. I'd like to stay here."

"Are you sure?"

"Yes . . . but I just . . . I just can't understand," she whispered. "I mean, I'm so happy that the boy's okay, but *how* did he survive this? How's it possible that he's not even injured?"

"I can't give a clear answer to that," said Stephen. "Perhaps at the last moment his mother changed her mind and pushed him away. Or maybe he was knocked from her arms and thrown to the side. I just can't be sure. But I do know that sometimes incredible things happen – things we can't explain. He's just really lucky I suppose."

"I know why he survived," said Tony. "It's like what my mother used to say to me when I was a boy back in Italy. She was a very religious woman, my mother, and she'd always say, 'God has a purpose for everything'. And I agree with her. I believe there's a *reason* why the boy was saved. God has a plan for him."

While Stephen spoke to Karen and the stationmaster, Peter had been sitting quietly with Ross on the other side of the office. He couldn't hear what they were saying, but he could see that Karen was upset and had been crying. Suddenly he jumped down from the chair and walked across the room.

"Hey, come back here," Ross called out; but it was too late, and he had made his way to the group and stood next to Karen. The conversation stopped as he unexpectedly joined them.

"Hi," said Stephen. "I'm sorry, we were forgetting about you, weren't we?"

The boy was staring at Karen, and it became obvious that he was thinking of something important but couldn't quite find the words.

"I want to say . . ." his tiny voice said softly.

"Yes," said Stephen. "What would you like to say?"

"My mummy . . ." He glanced at Stephen, then back at Karen again. "My mummy says we shouldn't cry." He slowly held out his hand and placed it on Karen's.

She took his hand, then leaned forward and kissed him gently on the forehead. "Thank you, Peter," she said. "You're very kind."

"You know," Stephen whispered to the stationmaster, "I think you're right – maybe there *is* a reason. I think there's something special about this boy." He bent down and carefully picked him up. "C'mon my little man. It's time to get you out of here."

As Stephen and Ross exited the office carrying their patient, they were met by their manager on the concourse. She introduced them to a Senior Constable who would accompany them to the hospital and continue to coordinate enquiries. Then they returned to the ambulance and drove to the emergency department, where they handed Peter over safely to the staff.

Karen stayed in the stationmaster's office for another two hours that afternoon while Tony continued to manage the situation. She insisted on completing all the necessary reports, and gave a full statement to the police.

By mid-afternoon her regional manager ordered her to go home and told her she had the next week off. The counsellor had been arranged and would visit her at home the next morning. A member of the highway patrol drove her home.

As Karen came through the front door, her mother looked up from the magazine she was reading in the lounge room. "Hello dear; you're home early," she said, as her daughter entered the room. "I wasn't expecting you till dinner time."

"Yes, I know mum. I got off early today."

"Is there something wrong? Did something happen?"

"Everything's alright mum, but it's been a bit of a strange day. Can I talk about it later?"

"Yes, of course."

"Where's Toby?" Karen asked.

"He's in his bedroom playing. He's been so well behaved this afternoon."

Karen smiled. "Good. I'll just go and see him."

She left the room and went down the hallway. As she entered the bedroom, she found her four-year-old son sitting on the floor. He was surrounded by his toy train set and was busy pushing a blue steam engine and several carriages around the wooden tracks.

"Mummy!" he said excitedly, as he looked up. "Mummy, I put the tracks together all by myself!"

"Yes, I can see you've done a wonderful job. Your train tracks look great."

"Sit down and play with me, mummy. Play with me, *please!*"

She sat down on the floor next to him and cuddled him tight. And when her mother came to check on them half an hour later, Karen was still sitting on the floor playing with her son by the train tracks.

Stephen was able to check on Peter a couple of times during the remainder of his shift. He remained well, and apparently everyone in the emergency department had fallen in love with him, including the police and social workers. Yet, his family was difficult to trace. Then, just prior to finishing, Stephen phoned the hospital and a nurse friend told him that the police had finally managed to locate his grandparents.

For the rest of his life, Stephen would remember the remarkable incident at Rivendell, and especially the dusty little boy he had lifted from the railway tracks. He would often imagine how the boy must be growing into a man, and then finding his way in the world.

Yet, as the years passed, Stephen's memory of the incident became increasingly vague and he could no longer recall the names of anyone involved. Although he may have passed him several times on the street, or even heard his name mentioned in the media, Stephen would never knowingly see or hear of the boy again.

* * * * * * * * * * *

Peter Schilling

Abridged extract – New York Times, August 10, 2093.

WORLD MOURNS LOSS OF GREAT SCIENTIST AND HUMANITARIAN

Professor Peter Schilling died peacefully in his sleep at his home in Lausanne, Switzerland this morning. He was 93 years old. After a sudden decline in health in early July, he spent four weeks at the Geneva University Hospital, but requested to go home last Monday so he could rest in the company of his family and close friends.

Peter Schilling is known internationally as the "Father of Pure Energy" and was born in Sydney, Australia in the year 2000. When only four years old, his father abandoned the family, and shortly afterwards, his mother died tragically in a railway incident. The young Peter was then raised by his grandfather, who was working as a senior lecturer in physics at the University of Sydney.

Schilling was an exceptional student at both school and university. By 2023 he had gained honours in physics, molecular science and advanced mathematics at Sydney. It was in 2028, however, that his name and work rose to world prominence. In that year he obtained his Ph.D. degree at the University of Cambridge and published a series of papers titled "New Directions in Energy", which immediately took the attention of the international scientific community.

This ground-breaking work not only incorporated his two famous formulas, but also proposed a number of innovative methods for the

43

efficient production of unlimited, safe and completely clean energy derived from sea water. He had effectively unlocked the door to a whole new era of world-wide energy production, which would drastically reduce the near critical effects of global warming at that time.

In 2029, he was awarded the Nobel Prize for both Chemistry and Physics. In the same year, he was invited to lead an international team based in Geneva, which developed the practical applications for the methods he had proposed. By 2033, the new 'Schilling Reactors' were being incorporated into existing power grids throughout the world.

It was during this period that he gained the respect of all world leaders by insisting that his discoveries and techniques would never be patented or gain royalties by any country or corporation. Rather, they should be freely shared by all nations on equal terms. He always maintained that it was his moral duty to create clean energy for humanity, and had no interest whatsoever in personal profit.

He was awarded the Noble Peace prize in 2035, and is generally regarded as the principal architect of energy production in the 21st Century.

His children report that their father had only one regret. He always wished that his mother could have known what he had achieved.

* * * * * * * * * * *

The Girl

Michael took the 18:03 train from Croydon and arrived in the city by half past. From the station to the theatre was a ten-minute walk, and he still had over an hour till the show started.

He and his wife had often seen shows in the city, but since she'd died, he hadn't been interested in doing much at all. For a long time, such things as musicals and concerts didn't have the same appeal. However, it had now been two years, and when he heard that Petula Clark was performing for the last time at the Capitol, he felt that old tug, and longed to be immersed in nostalgic memories of his youth in the sixties.

He left the stale, metallic-scented atmosphere of the busy railway station and made his way outside to the pedestrian concourse that ran down to the old park on Eddy Avenue. The cool winter evening remained damp and fresh after some earlier rain. The pavement glistened with the vivid reflections of city lights, broken by the chaotic movement of hundreds of pedestrians in the peak hour. The crawl and grind of city traffic was humming all around him.

Since he'd almost fallen asleep on the train, he bought a coffee from one of the small shops that line the concourse. Then he sat on a nearby bench where he could mix the warm coffee with the night air and survey the whole scene.

It was after a few sips that he first noticed the girl. She was about thirty metres away down the concourse, moving from bench to bench asking people for money. A businessman in a dark suit waved her away, and she patiently moved on. An old lady seemed to apologise to her, so she drifted casually to the next bench. Then a couple of construction workers gave her some change. She thanked them, then stepped away a little and began counting the coins.

She was now quite close to where he was sitting, and he guessed she was only fifteen or sixteen years old. He felt saddened that someone so young was out on the streets begging for money. She was slender, fair-skinned, and her dark hair was greasy and wet from the rain. Her clothing was covered in a generous quantity of the city's dust and grime, and thankfully included a thick jacket to protect her from the cold.

Although much younger, he was a little disturbed by how much she resembled his own daughter. Beneath the damp and dirt, it was really quite surprising how similar she looked. So, for a moment he was reminded of his latest misfortune. How unlucky, he thought, that his only child should head off overseas and fall in love with an American. "Come, visit us – you'll like San Francisco," his daughter had said many times. "Maybe I should," he said to himself.

When the girl turned towards him, he took another sip of coffee and watched her carefully as she approached.

"Have you got any change you can spare? I just want to buy a hamburger," she said in a somewhat subdued and routine fashion.

"A hamburger," Michael replied. "How much do you need?"

"I need five dollars, but I've only got three-fifty."

Now she stood next to him, he could see the differences between the girl and his own daughter. However, he remained intrigued by the qualities of her face. It was pale, quite dirty, and there were some light abrasions across her upper cheek and forehead. Her hazel eyes had little expression, and she spoke softly, with a tone that conveyed a deep tiredness.

He had seen this type of face before. It was built on abuse – perhaps physical or sexual, but certainly emotional – and it lay in a bed of neglect. Then, upon this foundation there was an encounter with the streets. He wondered how long she'd been out there. Had she found the shelter or the refuge, or spent nights in a car, a train or

46

a park? Had she joined a gang? She was living with the threat of alcohol and drugs, propositions from pimps, dealers and spruikers, and the force of the law. Although deep in the city, she lived on the dangerous fringe of society, where fear and anger walk constantly with the weak and vulnerable.

Yet, despite this, there was something else about this girl – something difficult to define. Below the veil of wet hair, dirt and abrasions, he sensed a certain kindness, hiding remorsefully.

"Here, take this," he said, reaching into his wallet and handing her a ten dollar note. "Get yourself a proper hamburger – one with the works. And get something to drink too."

She held it for several seconds, just staring at it in her hand. Then she looked up and whispered, "thank you." The gratitude in her response was mixed with surprise and just a little embarrassment. For the first time she gave a hint of a smile.

"You're welcome," he said.

"Thank you very much," she said again, and she turned and headed towards a kiosk on the other side of the concourse.

Michael had wondered whether she really wanted food or was collecting money for something else, so he kept his eyes on her. Sure enough, she bought what appeared to be a very large hamburger and a bottle of soft drink. Then she moved to a bench about twenty metres away, where she unwrapped the burger and started eating. He was surprised by her hunger, as she hardly took a breath till it was finished. 'God, she must have been starving,' he thought.

He considered the circumstances that had driven her to the streets. Where had she come from, and where was she heading? Did she have family, and did they care? She still seemed so innocent, but if this was so, he felt it wouldn't last long.

He remembered what his wife had said to him some years earlier. *"Michael, you can't change the world, but on any day, you might change the life of one person."* He realised it was so easy in the city to live a life without a single care for anyone around you. It was usually quite inconvenient to do otherwise.

As she sucked down the last drops of her drink, she glanced over and caught Michael watching her. She gave a small smile and raised the bottle in the air. Then, at that moment, without thinking further, he found himself walking across the concourse towards her. She looked on, somewhat warily as he approached. He figured she'd probably had men come to her before.

"You were obviously very hungry," he said.

She wiped the edges of her mouth with her hand. "Yes, I was; but I'm a lot better now."

"Well, I'm just glad you got a feed." He glanced down the concourse and drew a long breath, not too sure as to how he should proceed. "I suppose it's not easy being out here, is it?" he said finally.

"I'm doing okay," she replied, a little defensively.

"Yes . . . of course. Have you been in the city long?"

She hesitated for a moment. "A few months, I guess. Hey, what do you want?"

"I'm just wondering if you've found a safe place to stay."

"Look, I'm real grateful for your help with the food. But you don't need to help me anymore. I can take care of myself." She gave him a firm stare.

He was annoyed at himself. He hadn't started well – been too quick and intrusive.

"Yes . . . I understand," he said. "I'm sorry, I should have introduced myself. My name's Michael – I'm a social worker. I work here in the city, helping people. Maybe, if you want, I could help you get some better accommodation."

The girl grinned. "Oh, for a second there, I thought you were trying to get me back to your place. No, don't worry, I've already got a place with some friends."

He glanced again at the state of her clothes, and then down at her hands, which were just as grimy. He noticed her knuckles were bruised, and she'd lost the skin from a few. Wherever she was, it must be rough, he thought.

"Can I ask how old you are?" he enquired.

48

"I'm eighteen! I'm allowed to do what I want – right?"

"Yes, that's true." He didn't believe her – not for a moment – but he wasn't going to press the issue. "Tell me, this place you've got with your friends; are you happy there? Is it safe?"

"Sure . . . it's fine. It's all I need."

"But you know there are places in the city that are set up to help you. They've got facilities and people who can give you a hand. There's a shelter not far from here, with a women's section. They have a kitchen with free food."

"Yeah, I know it – that's a fuckin' awful place. I spent a night there and got most of my gear stolen. I can tell you, I'm not going back there!"

He thought for a second, nodding passively. "Yes . . . I'm sorry about that. Well, what about the women's refuge – that's just down in Lewisham. It's very safe and would be ideal for you."

She shook her head. "No, I don't want to go there either."

"You wouldn't consider it? It's only ten minutes away."

"No, my mates are here in the city. Besides, if you go there, they probably try to contact your family. I don't want that." She glared at the pavement and raised her voice a little. "My mum would say anything – make it sound like *I'd* done something wrong. As if I was to blame for *her* fuck-ups. Like her new boyfriend – he's a prick. There's no way – I don't want anyone telling me I should go home. Not with that dead-shit in the house."

Michael realised he had just brushed the surface of an open wound. She was more on edge than he had realised. In her face, he could see that perfect blend of fear and anger. It was there, simmering, ready to explode with the slightest irritation.

"So . . . back home, do you think they reported you missing? You know – with the police."

"Hah!" she scoffed. "My mum and that leech, Justin – I don't think so. There's no way they'd call the cops. Besides, who'd want them anyway? They never fuckin' help anyone."

49

He pondered for a second. "Hmm . . . I understand. Well, not the police, but did you ever get a chance to speak to someone else about things at home? Like, get some professional advice."

"No, not interested. I can deal with it. I'm not going to talk about it."

Michael took down the last of his cold coffee. He wasn't going to inquire any further. He had an idea of what was happening at home, and it was bad enough to make her escape. Now she was frightened of being sent back. She'd found a squat with some mates – probably one of the gangs – and she'd been lucky so far. Although she was begging, she didn't seem to be too affected by alcohol or drugs. But she lacked resources and her luck couldn't last. Soon she'd fall into a bigger trap and become another casualty.

"Fair enough," he said. "I won't talk any more about home . . . but I *can* offer you one thing. With my work, I deal with the women's refuge a lot. In fact, the director is a very good friend of mine. I'd really like to help you, so if you let me take you down there, I can explain things to her and make sure they don't try to contact your family. It's usually busy but I know we can arrange a bed, and you can settle in for a while. It's safe, clean, good food. And they can help you make some plans for the future, which don't involve going home. Does that sound okay?"

She looked away and shook her head. "No . . . it's better here in the city. Really, I'm doing fine."

He said nothing for a moment, as he considered her response. He could only do so much. "Well, I'm just trying to help," he said finally.

"Yeah, thanks for the offer, but I've got to go." She stared off down the concourse, as if she was looking for someone.

"Yes, I've got to go too," he said, glancing at his watch. "I'm off to see a concert – that's why I came in. But when it's finished, I'll be coming back here to the station. That'll be about eleven o'clock. So, please, could you at least think about it? If for any reason you change your mind – any reason at all – you'll find me standing here. I'll be right here at eleven o'clock. You understand?"

"Yeah, I understand," she said. "You've been kind, and I know you're trying to help . . . so don't worry, I'll think about it. But if I'm not here, don't wait around. Okay?"

"Yeah," he whispered with a small sigh, and he tossed his empty coffee cup into a rubbish bin by the end of the bench. "Well, thanks for talking to me. Maybe I'll see you later."

She said nothing, but continued to gaze into the dim heart of the concourse, still busy with the random movement of pedestrians.

He headed off towards the park. He didn't look back, but imagined she was still sitting there, deep in thought. He wondered what was going through her mind now. Was the conversation worth it? He couldn't be sure, but figured he'd done as much as he could.

As he reached the edge of the park, he turned and looked back. She was gone.

He was seated at the front of the dress circle, and had an excellent view of the stage. As Petula Clark walked out gracefully and stood before them, the entire audience rose in thunderous applause. Here was a woman, he thought, who had been in the limelight for almost her entire life. She had been supported, loved and respected by those around her throughout the years. Talented and fortunate, she had a clear definition of who she was. In his mind, she had always known exactly where she stood, and exactly where she was going.

Now well into her seventies, her voice was not as perfect as it had been, but that mattered little to the audience. She had the crowd captivated from the start, and they sang, swayed, cheered and reminisced their way through every moment of an outstanding performance.

As Michael had hoped, the concert regularly plunged him into pleasant memories of his younger days. Yet, despite this, all too often he was drawn back to thinking of the present. Just as his mind would drift and be absorbed by the brilliance of the lady on stage, or by the

51

power of the orchestra, thoughts of the girl would spring back to him. And classic hits such as 'Downtown' and 'Don't Sleep in the Subway' didn't help the situation. She was out there somewhere, in the company of God-knows-who, and the question of whether she would respond or not to his offer, became an inescapable intrusion on the evening.

When the concert finished, he made his way out to the street amongst the chatter and bustle of the theatre crowd. A long row of taxis stood waiting for business, as hundreds of excited people moved in all directions. Over the babble, he could hear the distant sound of sirens about the city. It was quarter to eleven, much colder, and he was grateful there had been no further rain.

The city was different now. As he left the area and walked towards the old railway station, the crowd quickly thinned. Soon, there were only a small number of people in sight – their scattered silhouettes moving silently past the illuminated fronts of offices and shops. The congestion and din of the peak period were well gone – replaced by the relative calm of the late hour on a chilly night. An intermittent car or bus would pass, and occasionally he found a small pocket of activity at a pub or night club, but otherwise, the hum of the city seemed rather distant. He enjoyed these moments, when there was a degree of peace and composure on the streets.

As he came around the park and looked toward the station, he saw a solitary police car parked in the middle of the concourse. Its hazard lights were on and a young police officer was sitting against the bonnet with his arms crossed. Another officer was standing about twenty metres away, talking to an old man while scribbling in his notebook. Otherwise, the area seemed almost empty, the shops were closed, and only a few pedestrians moved about the fringes. There was no sign of the girl.

Michael approached the police officer who was resting on the car. As he got near, the officer looked up at him and spoke. "I'm sorry sir, but you'll have to keep out of this area. If you could go around that way." He pointed to one side of the concourse.

"I was just wondering what happened," Michael said.

The officer sighed. "There was a brawl sir. Now, if you could keep going."

"Was anyone injured?"

"I can't really talk about it, sir. Now, as I said . . ."

Michael interrupted him. "Well, actually constable, you *can* talk about it." He pulled out his identification and showed it to the officer, who then quickly stood to attention.

"I'm sorry Chief Inspector, I didn't realize who you were."

"That's not a problem. Just tell me what happened."

"A fight broke out sir, about twenty minutes ago . . . between some kids. There was meant to be about four or five of them, but they'd all gone by the time we got here. Except for the one girl, who was badly injured. The paramedics were putting her in the ambulance as we arrived. They said it was serious and they've taken her to St. Vincents. She was stabbed in the face, sir. That's her blood right there." He pointed to the pavement, just a few metres in front of the car. Michael noted a large pool of fresh blood and a scattering of fine drops. "Our other crew followed the ambulance to hospital. We've called the detectives, sir, and also the Scientific Unit. Unfortunately, we've only got one witness that stayed. That's the man over there with my partner, but I think he's pretty drunk."

"You've done well," Michael said. "But tell me; you said the victim is a girl. Did you see what she looked like?"

"Not really, sir. As I said, the paramedics had her, and I only got a glimpse. She had a bandage on one side of her face, and an oxygen mask, but she looked quite young – maybe mid-teens."

"Was she fair-skinned with dark hair?"

"I'm sorry sir. Maybe she was, but I really can't be sure."

The other police officer had finished speaking to the witness, and was walking back to where his partner and Michael were standing.

53

As he approached, he finished a call on his phone. He was a senior constable, much older than his partner, and he recognised Michael.

"Good evening, sir. Nice of you to join us,"

"Oh, I won't be staying long. I'm just on my way home. I understand you have the detectives coming."

"Yes sir. I can see my partner has filled you in. I just got a call from Doug at the hospital. He's on the other car, sir. He says the victim is a sixteen-year-old female and she's been stabbed in the face. He had no chance to speak to her. Apparently, it's quite serious and they've taken her straight to surgery. That old bloke over there – he's not going to be much help, I'm afraid. He's too drunk and can't see very well. His descriptions are next to useless. Just says he saw a group of kids standing about, then there was a lot of shouting and they all ran off to the park. Then he saw the victim sitting on the ground screaming, and he came over and held his scarf against her face till the ambulance arrived."

"Hmm . . . not a bad effort. Have you got anyone searching the park?"

"Yes sir. I put out a call, and one of the anti-theft crews is searching now. But I don't think they'd be hanging round the park. Not after this. By now, the offenders could be anywhere."

"Is there any CCTV coverage of this area?"

"No, I'm afraid not. That only starts up there inside the station."

Michael shook his head in disappointment. "That's a pity." He glanced over at the old man. "This witness here – did he call the ambulance?"

"No sir, he doesn't have a phone. The call was anonymous. There must have been at least one other witness, but of course, they've gone. You know, not many people stay to talk to us at this time of night."

Michael nodded in agreement. "Yes . . . I understand. The injured girl – did you get a look at her before she left in the ambulance? Was she thin, with fair skin and dark hair?"

The senior constable thought for a moment. "Thin . . . yes. And she was a white Australian. But her hair – I don't know. Most of her head was covered in a bandage, so I couldn't say. Do you think you know her, sir?"

"Oh . . . I don't know . . . maybe. It's just a hunch. Do we have her details?"

"I don't have them. She was put in the ambulance, then she was gone. But I can call Doug back if you want. He can get them."

Michael thought for a moment. "No, that's not necessary. I'll call the detectives in the morning."

An unmarked police car pulled up at the bottom of the concourse. Two detectives got out and started walking towards them. Michael recognised them immediately, and didn't want to get tied up in further conversation.

"Alright," he said, "I'm going to leave it there. You've both done an excellent job. Tell them I'll give them a call tomorrow. We'll see what the outcome is on the girl, and if they've managed to gather anything on the offenders."

"Yes sir," said the senior constable.

Michael headed up the concourse towards the station entrance, his mind buried deep in thought. All he knew for sure was that a sixteen-year-old girl with a similar description had been seriously injured, and the perpetrators had escaped. Yet, he was more frustrated by what he didn't know. Was she there, waiting for him? Was she the victim? He really had no idea what the chances were. All she'd said was that she would *think* about it. Now, in a strange way, he preferred to believe that she never came back. The truth was, she hadn't seemed that interested. He tried to convince himself that she was well away, tucked up safe and sound in whatever God-damned place she'd found. However, in his heart there was a stronger conviction, and it niggled him. As much as he tried to assure himself otherwise, deep down he felt that it must have been her. She had been waiting there, ready to leave the streets and hoping for his assistance. She was waiting just as he had asked her to – willing to trust him and take the opportunity he offered. And now she was lying in a hospital, scarred for life. The thought irritated him sorely. God knows why she'd been targeted. Maybe for that very same reason – for telling her 'mates' she was getting out. He'd seen that in gangs before – these strange notions of loyalty. Each member has their own history, and the dynamics of gang life are always unpredictable.

For a moment, he thought of his daughter again. He figured it was now early morning in San Francisco, and soon she would be waking and getting ready for work. Didn't she tell him she took one of those old trams? He thought of how beautiful she was, and how much he missed her this last year.

As he entered the station, the musty surroundings of brick and steel, coated in murky-green fluoro, snapped him from his thoughts and brought him back to the present. He had resolved that there was little more he could do this evening. Better to go home, get some sleep, and phone the detectives in the morning. Then he could visit the girl in hospital, whoever she was. For now, he had to clear his mind, and he looked forward to relaxing on the train.

Her young voice came from behind him, and struck quite unexpectedly. "Michael! I'm here – it's me."

He looked around and saw the girl walking quickly towards him from just inside the entrance. He was elated, but suddenly questioned whether she'd seen him talking to the constables. Although he'd been a good fifty to sixty metres away and the lighting was poor, it was possible. If she had, surely, she couldn't have heard or seen much.

"Oh! You *are* here – thank God," he said. "There was a girl attacked down there on the concourse, just a short while ago. Did you know that? I've just been talking to the police because I thought it may have been you."

"No . . . look at me, I'm fine," she said. "I didn't know what was going on, but when I arrived there was a lot of cops hanging around down there, so I decided to come up here. I knew you'd be coming through. Are you still okay to take me to the women's refuge?"

"Yes! Of course, yes." He chuckled a little. "God, I'd managed to convince myself it must have been you. But here you are, perfectly safe. Thanks for coming back. I wasn't so sure you would. I'll take you there and help you settle in. Believe me, it'll be much better for you."

"Yeah . . . I thought about it. You're right – it's a better idea than staying in the city. Can we go?"

"Yes, let's go. Come on, I'll get you a train ticket."

They started walking towards the ticket machines.

"You know, you haven't told me your name," he said.

She didn't respond for a moment, but then said, "Sheri."

"Sheri?"

"Yeah, it's short for Sheridan."

"Hmm, well Sheri, did you tell any of your friends that you're going to the refuge?"

"No . . . I didn't want to talk to them – I don't need to. I just want to leave and not have to explain things to them."

"Yes, you're right – that's the best way."

As he put some coins into the machine, she stood back a little and watched on. "I saw you arrive," she said. "You seemed to know those coppers pretty well."

He hesitated briefly, and continued to stare at the machine. "No . . . I don't know them. But since I couldn't see you, I needed to ask them what happened." He took the ticket from the slot, and turned to her with a smile. "You know, with my work I do have to speak to the police every now and then. You understand."

"Yeah, but you don't have to tell them when you take someone to the refuge, do you?"

"No, not at all. That's just between you and me. Here – have a ticket."

There was only a dozen or so passengers sprinkled throughout the carriage, and they found an empty area down the end where they could both sit by the window facing each other. It was one of the

57

more modern trains – quite smooth and quiet on the tracks, good air-conditioning, and the carriage was well illuminated. Having run out of things to say, they both stared silently at the colourful city lights passing slowly in the darkness outside.

After a while, his eyes left the window and he began to study her more closely. Sitting so near, in the brightness of the carriage, gave him the clearest view he'd had all evening. She continued to gaze into the night, appearing deep in thought and occasionally whispering to herself. To him, she was obviously coming to terms with all the sudden changes in her life.

He noted a small tattoo of a blue butterfly on her upper neck, just under the ear, which he had not seen earlier. He wondered why kids these days were so interested in tattoos. At this stage, he preferred to think that she had never come to the attention of police before, but if she had, such a distinctive tattoo and her uncommon name, would easily identify her.

She was thankfully much drier than she had been earlier. Yet, she still bore all the grime and markings of her time on the streets. Once they got to the refuge, the staff would give her every opportunity to wash, and she'd get another meal if she wanted one. Her clothes could go to the laundry, and they'd find her some fresh ones for the time-being.

She had said she could take care of herself, and he had to admit, to a certain extent, she had. Still, where was the social justice when so many young were pushed to the streets? Over the years, he had seen hundreds of them out there. At least with this one, he hoped he could make a small difference.

He browsed at her hands as they lay peacefully in her lap. There were the same grazes on her knuckles that he had seen earlier, but her hands were somehow different. There was something odd. They seemed finer; more elegant in some way. What is it? he asked himself. Then he realised they were clean. They were both very clean – even the fingernails. She had washed them thoroughly.

58

Instinctively, he scanned the arms of her jacket, and stopped cold at the tail end of the right sleeve, just above the wrist. He looked away for a moment, staring down the carriage, collecting his thoughts, before looking back again. He had recognised it straight away. Although undetectable to the vast majority, especially as it lay on such dirty fabric, it was for him, quite unmistakable. He had spent eighteen years in Homicide before he went to Special Branch, and he'd studied this pattern many times. A delicate spray of fine blood particles, almost like the imprint of a mist, now dried to a tone of mid-brown upon the sleeve. It was entirely consistent with the fine spray that comes at the very moment a deep, penetrating knife wound is delivered to uncovered flesh.

His heart sank and he suddenly felt very weary. What a waste, he thought, and such a tragic game to play. Damn the abusers that drive these kids to the streets and a life on the edge. God only knows what had happened back there on the concourse – there could be a thousand scenarios. But now he should be cautious, even though it was most unlikely she still had the knife. It could be anywhere back at the scene, but if she had carried it into the park, it would probably be in the pond, where she had no doubt washed her hands.

It was bitter compensation that, as an officer, he should now somehow feel grateful. Because in her search for a sanctuary, and in trusting him too much, she had made all his efforts seem so worthless. And now, all he could feel was the unforgiving hollowness of duty.

He resolved that nothing would be done on the train. He would wait till they arrived at the refuge and he had spoken privately to the director. When she was given a bed and a change of clothes, he would secure her jacket, pants and shoes for the forensic team. Then he'd call the detectives.

He glanced again briefly at the butterfly tattoo, and she turned from the window to face him. She seemed a little apprehensive, but then smiled and asked, "What concert did you go to?"

He did his best to be reassuring. "Petula Clark, at The Capitol. Do you know her?"

She thought for a second, her expression blank, then shook her head lightly.

They both gazed into the night once more. In the darkness he pictured his daughter sitting by the open window of an old tram with the wind in her hair, looking out across San Francisco Bay. He could see himself there beside her, laughing, with his arm around her shoulders, the clatter and bell of the tram resonating in his ears.

* * * * * * * * * * *

The Storyteller

The old man was resting in the dimly-lit lounge room when the doorbell rang. He got up slowly, steadied himself on the edge of the sideboard and walked to the window. He opened the blinds, filling the room with soft, dusty light, then quietly returned to the couch. Down the hallway, he could hear his wife shuffle from the kitchen to the front door, then the warm greeting to their daughter and their two young grandchildren. After more chatter and some laughter, the little ones asked, "Where's Grandad?" His wife mumbled something, then the children ran down the hallway and burst into the room.

They loved visiting their grandparents. The shady house was filled with old, dark furniture, peculiar ornaments and strange smells. And this was the time *he* loved the most. Now, in his eightieth year, all the others were grown up and too busy with their lives. So, these two young ones were very precious.

The boy was six and his sister was ten. "Grandad, we came to see you!" the girl said, and she and her brother gave him a cuddle and settled on the couch beside him.

"Thank you for that," he said. "I hope you can stay for a while."

"We're staying for lunch!" said the boy.

The old man smiled and nodded slowly.

The children looked about the room, and then the girl's gaze returned to her grandfather. "Tell us another story, Grandad," she said.

"Yes, I want a story too!" said the boy.

Immediately his wife called out from the kitchen. "Eric, lunch is in twenty minutes. That's *twenty!* – not twenty-five or thirty!"

The old man raised his eyebrows at the children. Whenever she used his name, he knew she meant business. "Yes," he called back. "I think I remember what twenty is. Thank you dear."

He glanced at his wristwatch, then put his arms around the children and said, "So, do you want a story from the *desert*, from the *mountains*, or from the *sea*?"

They thought for a few seconds, and were just about to answer when their mother appeared in the doorway. "Hi dad, how are you?" she said.

"Oh, hello Grace. I'm fine – just about to tell a story."

"Yes, that's good dad . . . and you know I love you dearly, but this time, please don't scare the children. After your last story, they didn't sleep for days. So, no stories from the war, okay."

"Yes, yes . . . I understand."

She blew them all a kiss, then turned and headed back to the kitchen.

"So, I guess that rules out anything from the desert," he whispered to the children.

The girl held his hand tightly. "Grandad, I want a story from the mountains."

"Yes, the mountains!" said the boy, sitting upright on the edge of the couch.

"Alright . . . let me see," said the old man, deep in thought. His eyes wandered to the window and he focused on the garden outside. On the branch of a nearby tree he could see two small robins, and for a moment they sat next to each other, tweeting and looking about. Then, one suddenly flew off, and a few seconds later, the other followed.

"Hmmm . . ." he murmured. "I think I've got one. It's an old story from before the wars. Haven't thought of this one for a long time."

"Oh, I like these old stories," the girl said eagerly.

"C'mon Grandad, start!" said the boy.

Then they sat beside their grandfather in silence, their eyes wide with anticipation, until he began.

"Once, many years ago, in the early 1900s, there were *two* brothers. Their names were Daniel and Gian. They lived in a village, way up in the Swiss mountains in the heart of Europe, where their parents owned a small grocery shop by the village square. And the really interesting thing about these two brothers is they were twins . . . and more than that, they were *identical* twins. So, of course, they looked exactly the same – you understand?"

Both children nodded rapidly. The old man settled back further into the couch, then continued.

"As this story goes, all through their childhood and up to the time when they were young men, Daniel and Gian remained very close friends. Also, they loved being seen as identical twins. In fact, throughout the district where they lived, they were famous for it. Because, not only did they look exactly the same, but they also cut their hair the same, and they always dressed the same. Since they made themselves look identical, it was generally accepted that only their parents could tell them apart. And, because they were such close friends, they did almost everything together. Whether they were at home, working in the village, out in the fields, or hiking in the mountains, they were always together. It was like they were two halves of the same person, and they understood that they would never let anything separate them.

Now, the brothers were raised properly, and they were cheerful, kind and adventurous. So, of course, there were a few occasions during their teenage years when they attracted the romantic attention of some of the girls from their village. But the fact that they were identical and could never be separated, always presented problems. The girls usually found their relationships with them became too confusing and difficult, and they didn't last long."

The old man smiled at his granddaughter. She gave a small chuckle, while her younger brother stared ahead in silence.

"Such failed relationships were not really a problem for Daniel and Gian, because they were always so content with their own company and the strength of their friendship.

However, when they were about 19 years of age, there came a time when a new family settled in the village. The old baker had finally retired and gone to live with his sister down in the valley. A new baker and his wife had quickly taken the lodgings above the bakery, and were soon hard at work producing a variety of fine bread. Every family in the village would buy their bread from the bakery, and soon all the folk became acquainted with the new baker, his wife, and the third member of the family – their charming 18-year-old daughter, Renate.

From the moment the brothers met Renate, a great friendship developed between the three of them. Both Daniel and Gian found her very beautiful, and she had an independent nature and a wit that set her apart from the others in the village. And while Renate thought the identical twins were a little unusual, she also found this quirkiness quite intriguing. Their modesty, good humour, and adventurous spirit, all suited her perfectly.

Before long, they were spending a lot of time together. On Wednesdays they would meet at the markets, and on Sundays they would sit together in church. On a few occasions they were seen walking in the mountains, and often, in the evenings, they would dance and share music in the village square. She would regularly visit the brothers at their family store, and many times, they came to help in the bakery. Although Renate's parents were a little cautious of the relationship at first, they were happy for the assistance, and soon became very fond of them.

As the months went on, it became clear to Daniel and Gian that they both shared a deep love for the same woman. Renate's heart too, was torn between her great love for each of them. Yet, underlying all this was an unspoken fact – the three of them quietly realised that the relationship was impossible. The brothers knew they couldn't continue to share a life with the one woman, and Renate could not contemplate having to choose one of the twins and splitting their special bond.

One day, Renate announced that she had decided to leave the village. She said she wasn't one for continuing the business of baking in the mountains, and looked forward to new life in the city, with all the great opportunities it offered.

Although her decision created great sadness for her parents and the two young men, they accepted it graciously, and on the day of her departure they all gathered to bid her farewell. As her carriage waited, Renate embraced her parents with tears in her eyes, and said she would write often. She then gave to each brother, a small gift – an identical neck chain and locket. When they opened their lockets, they each found one half of a picture of her face. One brother had the left side, and the other had the right. Renate told them, "You will both have half of me, and that way, together, you will still have the whole of me." Then she got into the carriage and was gone."

The old man took a short break from his story and looked down at the children. "So, do you understand what a *locket* is?"

"Yes," said the girl. "It's like a small metal case that has a picture in it, and it hangs around your neck."

"Yes, that's exactly what it is. But in this story, the two lockets have just *half* a picture each."

"Yes, Grandad, we know," said the boy. "Keep telling the story!"

The old man took a deep breath. "Ah, where was I? Oh, yes. Renate arrived in the city on the following day and took a small apartment near the centre. By the end of the week she was offered work in a large commercial bakery nearby. Soon, she had a small group of friends, and during her free-time she would explore the parks and venues of her new home.

Each week she wrote to her parents about how busy and exciting her new life was. Secretly, though, there was a deep sorrow in her heart, for she missed the mountains terribly, and thought daily about the twin brothers she loved so much. Sometimes, men from the city would show an interest in her, and although she remained social, she would never allow a relationship to develop.

Back in the mountain village, Daniel and Gian missed their girlfriend very much, and they remained sad for many weeks. Renate's parents allowed them to read every letter she sent home, and they believed, from the way she wrote, that she was very content. With friends and a good job, she appeared to have settled well into her new city life. So, slowly, with time, the brothers began to accept the situation, and they went back to their old routines and moved on with their lives.

Now, several months after Renate left, on a fine day in late summer, Daniel and Gian went on a long hike, high into the mountains. Many kilometres from their village, they found a remote valley they had not visited before. It had the most beautiful and dramatic scenery they had ever seen, and slowly carving its way through the valley's centre, was an enormous *glacier*." The old man looked down at the children again. "You understand? A glacier is a massive sheet of solid ice, very long and very deep, that is often found in the high mountain areas."

The children stared back at their grandfather, wide-eyed and nodding quickly.

"Okay then. So, being adventurous in nature, the brothers wished to explore the valley further, but to do so, they needed to cross a section of the glacier. They found the ice was very rugged, with many jagged ridges and troughs, so they took great care as they made their way steadily across. But suddenly there was a shudder, and a loud groaning and grinding sound from way below the surface. Then the glacier roared like thunder and split open violently, leaving the brothers clambering at the very edge of a wide crevasse – a huge and seemingly bottomless crack in the ice – that carved down deep into the heart of the glacier.

Daniel just managed to gain a strong hold of the ice, and he reached out for Gian, who was hanging precariously over the edge, straining to hold on, just a metre away. For a moment they clasped hands and each looked painfully into the eyes of the other. But then Gian slipped further, and his weight tore his hand from Daniel's grip. As he fell, Gian called out just one word to his brother – "stay!" Then he disappeared into the eerie darkness of the void below.

Daniel was left leaning over the precipice, screaming "Gian!" time after time, wretchedly, till he could scream no more. At every call, the pitiless glacier responded with complete silence – not the slightest sound from below – only that of Daniel, as he remained in solitary despair on the ice above.

He stayed there for hours, calling, till the sun disappeared behind the ridges, and the cold air bit hard at his face. He had never felt so utterly alone in his whole life. On several occasions he thought of throwing himself into the chasm – it would have been so easy. But then the last word of his brother rang in his head, again and again.

Finally, Daniel could do no more. He knew the situation was hopeless. He left the glacier, and spent a miserable and restless night sheltering in the forest. As soon as he had light on the following day, he trekked back to the village and, exhausted and distressed, informed his family and friends. Word spread quickly, and soon the whole village was in a state of shock.

A climbing team with long ropes was organised, and on the next day, Daniel led them back to the valley. They made their way onto the glacier and crossed the jagged ice, each man roped to the next in a long chain. Occasionally they stopped in fear as the glacier groaned and trembled below their feet. It was obvious to all that it was too unstable and constantly changing. They felt like tiny insects crawling on the back of a giant sleeping beast – an unpredictable beast that could wake at any moment.

Through their loyalty to Daniel, they stayed on the ice a lot longer than they wished to. But as much as they searched, in every direction, the crevasse could not be found. The ice was moving too often, and it had been closed. Gian had been swallowed and his body could not be retrieved. Painfully, slowly, they made the long trek home.

Daniel sorely grieved the loss of his twin brother, with whom he had shared so many adventures. The whole village, too, was in mourning, and hundreds came from all around the district to attend his memorial. The church was full to overflowing. Daniel sat at the front with his parents and closest friends. The baker and his wife were there too. They told him they had sent word to Renate, but had not heard anything in reply.

As everyone sat in silence, the priest spoke of love, sacrifice, and the power of God's healing. When it was done and all the words were said, the congregation came forward and extended their deepest sympathy to Daniel and his parents. Then they all slowly left the church. In the end, his parents also departed, and Daniel was left alone, sitting before the altar. Everything was still and perfectly silent, just like on the glacier.

He looked up and gazed upon the old wooden carving of Jesus on the cross. He had seen this almost every week of his life, but now, for the first time, he realised how truly painful and lonely it must have been. As the tears began to well in his eyes once more, he felt a light touch on his shoulder. He turned and found her gentle hand resting there. Then he stood and looked deeply into her beautiful, caring eyes. They embraced as they had never done before, and for several minutes, each wept openly onto the shoulder of the other."

"Was it Renate?!" asked the boy.

"Of course it was," said the girl. "Keep going Grandad – keep going."

The old man smiled at the children. Then he paused for a moment, closed his eyes, and gathered his thoughts.

"Renate never returned to the city. She stayed in the mountains she loved so much, and from that day forward, she and Daniel devoted their lives to each other. In the next spring they were married, and once again, the small village church was full to overflowing. They continued to live full and happy lives together and they raised a family, but they never forgot the brother they loved so dearly.

Every year, on the anniversary of Gian's death, they would return to the valley and stand by the glacier. And as they grew older and the world around them changed, each year they would stand there by the glacier and notice the mountains, too, were changing. The amount of snow on the peaks, the depth of the forest below, the roads and the clearings – all changing – just a little, year by year. And inch by inch, the mighty river of ice crept steadily onwards, down through the valley.

Many years passed, and the village became a thriving town. Daniel and Renate continued to live there till they were some of the oldest and most cherished members of the community. They were now too old to hike in the mountains, but were content to stay in the town, spending their time with family and friends.

One day, they were contacted by the local police and then driven to the base of that very same glacier, high in the mountains. There, at the bottom of the glacier, resting behind a wall of melting ice, lay the body of Gian. He could clearly be seen, fully clothed and intact, just the way he had been all those years before. He remained frozen in time, still the young man who had once been so identical to his brother.

Daniel and Renate gazed upon the scene and embraced each other closely. Gian seemed to be lying there so peacefully, one could almost see a smile on his face. His eyes were turned to the heavens, and one arm was outstretched toward the surface of the ice, as if he was reaching for something. Or, was he giving something away? As Daniel and Renate looked closely into his open hand, they could just make out the shape of a small chain and locket."

The old man had finished his story. He waited for a few moments, staring contentedly across the room, and then looked down at the children.

The girl was watching him inquisitively. "Is that a true story, Grandad?"

69

He gave a small chuckle in reply, and checked his wristwatch once more. "Oh look," he said. "That's twenty minutes. She'll be calling any second now."

A few seconds later, his wife's voice emanated from the kitchen. "Lunch is ready now!"

The young boy jumped off the couch, shot out the door, and ran down the hallway shouting excitedly. "Mummy, mummy, there were two brothers and they loved the same woman, but then one of them fell inside a glacier and he was covered in ice, and then he was *dead!* Then the woman married the other one, but after a really, really long time, the dead one came out of the ice again!"

"Oh, Jesus," the old man whispered to himself. "I think I'm going to be in trouble again."

The young girl wrapped her arms around her grandfather and hugged him tightly. "Don't worry, Grandad. I love your stories."

She hopped off the couch and went to the door, then turned to him again. "You'll always tell us stories, won't you Grandad?"

The old man smiled as he got up slowly. "I'll do my best, Sophie. I'll do my best."

* * * * * * * * * *

A Mouse Named Cloud

To my beautiful children.
May you have the good fortune to fully develop your talents,
and then the courage to display them on life's grand stage.

* * * * * *

Far away in the country, there was a small farm,
And there, by a brook, stood an old wooden barn.
Although it was rustic and seemed rather quaint,
The barn was quite broken and needed a paint.
It had rot in the walls and a rickety door,
The roof was leaking and there were holes in the floor.
It had cobwebs on the rafters and the smell was not nice,
For, above all, it was now a home for the mice.

There were mice in their hundreds, they were found everywhere –
In the roof, in the corners, and under the stair.
Fat ones, skinny ones, fast ones and slow,
Mice that stayed high and mice that stayed low.
Black ones, brown ones, white ones and grey,
Mice that liked seed and mice that liked hay.
And each mouse was *quiet* – they disturbed not a thing,
. . . except for the one that had learned how to sing.

There was one fluffy, white mouse who'd discovered her voice,
And she sang all the time because that was her choice.
Her tone, one would say, had a rather high pitch,
But was clear and refined, and really quite rich.
And she sang about grain and the things that mice chew,
Of dirt, wood and straw, and all the things that mice do.
She sang of the barn and how she had grown,
Because life in the barn was all she had known.

But the other mice said, "You're not one of us.
You're not '*quiet as a mouse*' – you're causing a fuss.
It's quite plain to see you don't fit in with this crowd.
You're singing too much; you're singing too loud.
And your voice is so high, it's a pain in the ear.
You're no longer welcome – we don't want you here."
So, the mice had a vote, and the vote said '*no more*',
And they scurried and bustled her right out the door.

The old farmer sat on his veranda all day,
Since his wife had passed on, and his kids moved away.
He was lonely and tired of working the farm.
Life on the land had lost all its charm.
Now, his only companion was an old radio,
And he listened to opera, and sang soft and slow.
That was all that he had – his music and the house,
When suddenly he was confronted by a small, singing mouse.

"Dear farmer," sang the mouse, "may I please stay with you?
I've been tossed from the barn; I don't know what to do."
"Oh yes," said the farmer. "You're most welcome here.
I've been so alone for more than a year.
A friend's what I need – a good friend who sings.
You may stay in my house, but remember two things:
Here we sing opera, because I'm quite a fan,
And please don't call me 'farmer' – my real name is Stan."

"I'm so grateful," sang the mouse, and to the farmer she bowed.
"I'm now your good friend, and *my* name is Cloud.
Yes, that's what they call me, and I must tell you why.
See, I'm so white and fluffy . . . and I sing way up high."
"But, what's *opera?"* she asked. "What is this strange word?
You said we sing 'opera'. This thing, I've not heard."
"Well, *opera's* my love," said Stan with a smile.
"Come, sit with me now and let's listen a while."

So, the two of them sat on the veranda each day,
And they sang with the radio as the months whiled away.
Together they sang opera like never before,
And Cloud found that her life could be filled with much more.
She learned that love was the essence of life,
And she learned about peace, then learned about strife.
She discovered that courage can walk beside fear,
And she found that one's joy was never far from a tear.

And as the radio played and they both sang along,
Cloud mastered the arias with a voice, high and strong.
Her voice was so pure – in fact it was superb,
And Stan thought it was the best soprano voice he'd ever heard.
But after several months, there came a fateful day,
When their dear old radio broke, and it simply wouldn't play.
And Cloud asked her close friend, "What are we to do?
It will break my heart if I no longer sing with you."

Stan thought long and hard, and looked out across his land.
He realised that the course of life is never as you planned.
"Dear friend," he said, "on this veranda we'll no longer sit.
If the opera cannot come to us, then we must go to it.
There's a place I've heard of and always wished to see –
A strange building in Sydney town, way down by Circular Quay."
So, they packed their bags and headed off across the plain.
By dusk they made the station, then caught the evening train.

73

The train pulled in to Circular Quay just before sunrise,
And as our two friends looked about, they couldn't believe their eyes.
Buildings of every shape and size rose up and touched the sky.
Mighty skyscrapers of concrete and glass – majestic, broad and high.
But one fantastic building stood out amongst the crowd.
Like a massive set of sails, it stood there grand and proud.
So, they found a room above a pub and left their bags secure.
"C'mon," said Stan. "Come with me. We're going to take a tour."

The opera theatre was deserted, as they entered with their guide.
They'd never seen a room so vast, so towering and wide.
Then on the distant stage, a single woman walked into sight.
With grace and poise she stood there within a pool of light.
"You're in luck," whispered the guide. "This is our treasured Dame.
Our most respected diva – a woman of great fame.
We must sit here, still and quiet, or we will have to go.
Soon she'll start rehearsing for her final show."

The treasured Dame looked up and then began to sing,
With a voice of power and beauty – a most enchanting thing.
But suddenly Cloud's ears pricked up, as she recognised the song.
Then she jumped up on her seat and started to sing along.
"Hush!" said the guide. "Be quiet – you must not interrupt.
This is a rehearsal that we should not disrupt."
But Cloud would *not* be stopped, and she continued loud and clear.
And Stan could not stop smiling as he wiped away a tear.

Cloud matched the diva note for note, as they continued their duet.
The woman on stage, the mouse in the stalls – neither was finished yet.
The Dame's voice soared to dizzy heights, and Cloud pursued her there.
Up where voices rarely go – where few sopranos dare.
They sang in perfect harmony; they bonded firm and proud,
And as their duet ended, they faced each other and bowed.
Then the Dame called out, "Who's singing there? Don't worry, I'm not upset.
Please come up here into the light. I think it's time we met."

Stan picked up Cloud and held her high, as he walked towards the Dame.
He placed her carefully on the stage, then heard his friend proclaim:
"Madam, it is I that sang, and I'm only a mouse, it's true,
But it has been a privilege to have this chance to sing with you."
"Yes," said the Dame, "you *are* a mouse – on this we're all agreed.
But you're an *opera mouse* with a very fine voice – a very fine voice indeed.
And for giving me such pleasure, I'll see you at my final show.
You're invited as my special guests, and you'll sit in the front row."

"So, I do hope you can be here – it's on this Saturday night.
And I promise you a show that will fill you with delight.
I'll be singing all the songs that gave me happiness and fame.
All the well-known arias that made me a household name."
"Oh yes!" said Cloud excitedly. "These songs I do recall.
I've sung them many times with Stan. I've memorised them all.
We will be here on the night – on that you can be certain.
And I promise you that I'll be quiet, until your final curtain."

Cloud and Stan toured the city as the next few days went past.
Then the big night came and they took their seats at last.
The theatre was completely full – there was only standing room,
And many people round them carried flowers in full bloom.
There were celebrities and bigwigs, and all the opera loyals.
And a rumour went around, there were even a couple of royals.
Then suddenly, as they sat there, they were approached by the theatre page.
He said, "Cloud and Stan, come quickly please. You're wanted now backstage."

They were taken through a stage door, then to a dressing room,
And there they met the treasured Dame, dressed-up in fine costume.
"My friends," she said with a husky voice, "I cannot sing a note.
I've got a sniffle in my nose, and a terribly sore throat.
Dear Cloud, you must sing for me – you have the talent, I know.
We cannot let the public down – we must not stop the show.
If you have the courage to stand with me before this massive crowd,
Then I'll have the courage to mime the words while you sing high and loud."

"What an honour," Cloud replied, "to place such faith in me.
I shall now repay this trust, and prove my loyalty.
I'm somewhat nervous, I'll admit, but now I must be brave.
This is now my mission – your show I'm going to save.
If I may sit upon your shoulder and hide there on your shawl,
The audience shouldn't see me, since I'm fluffy and small.
Stan, go back to your seat my friend, and worry not for me.
Dear Dame, our audience is waiting – let's fulfil our destiny!"

The performance was stupendous – it was dazzling and bright.
The treasured Dame seemed faultless as she sang into the night.
And as the concert ended, the crowd rose to its feet.
Never had they witnessed such an operatic treat.
Amid thundering applause, flowers rained upon the stage.
The critics all proclaimed it the best performance of the age.
But some commentators were perplexed – was it all some kind of bluff?
As the Dame spoke to reporters, her voice seemed hoarse and rough.

On the following day the three of them were sitting by The Quay.
Cloud was sipping milk, while the Dame and Stan had tea.
"Dear Cloud," said the Dame, "you could easily be a star."
"That's very kind," Cloud replied, "but I prefer things as they are."
"Well, somehow I must thank you for saving my final show.
Why don't you come and live with me in my old chateau."
"I'd gladly come," said Cloud, "if I can bring my good friend Stan.
He's given me so much, and he is your greatest fan."

"Now I'm retired," the Dame declared, "I need a good man in my life."
"What great luck," said Stan with a grin, "because I need a singing wife."
The Dame and Stan became close friends, and he offered her his hand.
And they had the finest wedding seen throughout the land.
They tied the knot on stage, inside the Opera House,
And *his* best man and *her* bridesmaid, was the same white, fluffy mouse.
And from time to time you'll hear them, should you wander by The Quay.
A Dame, a farmer, and a mouse named Cloud, singing happy as can be.

* * * * * * * * * * *

The Playground in the Park

Dedicated to the children.

Chris had just turned five years old and was very excited. He sat in his child seat in the rear of the family sedan and eagerly looked out the window as the city buildings passed by. His mother, Kate, and his grandfather, Bill, sat contently in the front. As Kate drove the car steadily onwards, Bill would sometimes look back at him and smile encouragingly.

For his birthday, they had told him they would take him somewhere very special. Now he was trying desperately to guess *where*. They had said it was a place he would definitely love to go, and that he hadn't been there before because they had to wait until he was old enough. Now they were playing a guessing game as the car got closer and closer to its destination, and his excitement was immense.

When he first saw the city in the distance, he had guessed it might be the new water-play park at Darling Harbour. "No, it's not there," Kate had said. "You've been there before. We took you last year – remember?"

Then he guessed they might be going on one of the really big harbour ferries. That was something he had always wanted to do. But, once again, his mother said it wasn't that. "It's much better than that," Bill had said.

Now, they were driving onto the Sydney Harbour Bridge, and suddenly a thrilling idea popped into the small boy's head. "Is it a place near the water that has a really big smiling face?" he asked, barely able to contain his anticipation.

"Yes!" Kate and Bill cried out together.

"And it's got lots of fun rides?!"

"Yes!" they exclaimed again.

"What's it called?! What's it called?!" he asked excitedly, while bouncing in his seat.

"Luna Park!" shouted Bill, sounding a little excited himself.

"Yes! Luna Park! That's what I always wanted!" the little boy screamed.

Chris took a firm hold of his mother's hand as they walked towards the iconic entrance of the park. Until this moment he had only occasionally seen the large smiling face in the distance, but now he was very close and confronted with its true size. A degree of apprehension stirred within him. The bright, colourful face towered above them, and its immense, blue eyes were staring directly at him. He suddenly realised that he would have to walk through its mouth, below the huge row of menacing white teeth. He reached out and grabbed his grandfather's hand as well. Then he pulled him and his mother in very close as the giant red lips and enormous teeth passed directly overhead.

Once swallowed, the amusement park stretched out before him as far as he could see. Its sights, sounds and smells relentlessly invaded his senses. He immediately saw the giant Ferris wheel pasted against the blue sky, and then the brightly coloured carousel below it. The grinding sound of old-fashioned carnival music was suddenly mixed with dozens of piercing screams emanating from somewhere in the distance. The vivid lights of stalls, and the bizarre, dreamlike facades of the other rides seemed to encompass him. Hundreds of animated people were passing in all directions. Other children, their faces sticky with ice-cream and fairy floss, skipped past, dragging their parents to places unknown. Their constant movement and noise surrounded him as the dazzling machinery of the amusement park was rising, turning and spinning everywhere he looked.

Chris stood motionless beside his grandfather in the middle of the concourse. He said nothing, but remained wide-eyed and open-mouthed, taking it all in. Without warning, a large, magical clown with a white face, flaming orange hair and a huge red nose appeared before him. "Welcome to Luna Park little man," said the clown, with a huge grin.

Chris was too surprised to speak, and he tightly embraced his grandfather's leg.

"It's alright Chris – it's just a clown," said Bill. "This is his first time at Luna Park," he continued to say to the clown.

"Oh, this is your *first* time," said the clown, and he bent down closer to the boy. "And what is your name my little friend?"

"Chris," he replied, still holding fast to Bill's leg.

"Well, Chris, I wish you a day full of wonder and surprises. Maybe I'll see you later on, and I'll ask you how you went." The clown looked up briefly and winked at Bill.

"Thank you," said Bill, and the clown turned and strode off in the direction of other newcomers.

Chris looked about and realised that his mother was not with them. "Where's Mummy?" he asked.

"She's just over there," Bill said, pointing at the nearby ticket counter. "She's been getting our tickets. Here, come with me and we'll go and see her."

Kate let out a small sigh as they joined her at the counter. "Dad, I've been trying to call you but you couldn't hear me."

"Sorry dear, but Chris and I have been talking to a clown. Did you see him?"

"Ah . . . no, I didn't. I've been trying to organise these passes. Now listen – Chris has to stand against this height chart. I think he's about one hundred and ten centimetres, so he should get a green pass. He's not allowed to go on *all* the rides, but we didn't want that anyway. Some of them are far too scary." She helped Chris stand against the height chart. "Now stand up nice and straight so the man can see you."

Chris stood as tall as he could and stared, straight-faced, at the young man dressed in the strange uniform behind the counter.

"Yes, he gets a green pass," confirmed the man. "So, would you all like a green pass, or are you going to do a few of the bigger rides by yourself?"

"Oh no – just three green ones will do nicely," Kate replied with a chuckle.

She paid the man and they fastened their passes around their wrists. Then Kate took her son's hand and the three of them headed slowly over the bustling concourse.

"So, this is all I need – this little green wrist band?" Bill enquired.

"Yes Dad, that's all you need," Kate said, a little amused. "They don't use tickets anymore."

Bill gazed widely about the park. "So much has changed since I last came here," he said. "I think the last time I was here was in the early seventies, when I was still a teenager. We used to come here quite a lot. Back then, you could buy a whole roll of tickets for a couple of bucks. We'd try to sneak into some of the rides without using one. God, we had a lot of fun. I can't believe it's been over forty years!"

"Yes, everything's changed since those days. But they had to improve the place, didn't they? I've seen some photos of the old park – it was falling apart." Kate turned to one side and whispered in her father's ear. "And I heard they had some accidents back then."

"Oh, yes," Bill whispered back. "I remember them *very* well. It was the main reason I never brought you here when you were young. They happened in seventy-nine, just after you were born. First, there was a crash on the Big Dipper, and a lot of people were injured. And, as if that wasn't bad enough, then they had a really big fire in the Ghost Train, and quite a few were killed."

"Killed? I didn't realise there were deaths."

"Yes – it was a big story, and very sad. I remember there was a father and his two young boys; and there was another group of school boys as well. They all died in the fire – it was just terrible. They

80

closed the park for a number of years after that. When they reopened, your mum and I had lost interest in the place."

Chris looked up inquisitively at his mother, and then pulled at her arm. "What are you and Granddad whispering about?" he asked.

"Oh, nothing much," said Kate, smiling warmly at her son. "Just talking about the good old days, when Granddad came here as a boy." She looked back at her father. "Well, anyway, what I was thinking was that we shouldn't go on any rides that are *too* scary."

"Yes, I agree," said Bill.

"Can we go on *that* ride?" Chris asked, pointing up at the Ferris wheel.

"Yes, of course," said Kate. "We're definitely going on that ride – it's one of the best. But, can we keep that one till last? I'd like to finish off with the Ferris wheel because it's very special." She squatted down next to her son, and pointed to the top of the wheel. "You see all the way up there. From up there we'll have a great view across the whole park, and the harbour too. So, it's nice to do it at the end of the day. Is that alright with you?"

"Yes Mum; but make sure you don't forget. I really want to go on that one."

"Okay, I promise – I won't forget." She quickly glanced around the park. "But for now, why don't we start on the carousel. It's just over there."

"Yes, come on, let's go!" Chris yelled excitedly, pulling his mother's arm in that direction. "I want to go on all the rides!"

Chris was lifted by his grandfather onto one of the vividly coloured horses. The saddle felt a lot harder than he had expected, and he held on firmly to the pole. "Can you stay with me Granddad?" he asked, a little anxiously.

"Yes, of course I can," said Bill, and he placed a hand on the boy's shoulder.

As they rode the carousel, round and round, Kate stood just outside the fence and watched them with great interest. She took a

81

couple of photos, then waved and cheered each time they passed. With each rotation she was delighted to see that her son's confidence was growing. His face was lighting up, and his smile broadening.

When the ride came to an end, Chris turned to his grandfather and said, "Again! Again! Can I go again Granddad?"

"Yes, I don't see why not," said Bill. "But I want to watch you from down there with your mother, okay? I'm starting to get a little dizzy. So, just hold on tight. You'll be right, I'm sure."

As the carousel started up once more, Bill joined his daughter outside the fence and they looked on together. Kate waved again to her small son, who held on tight and beamed back at them.

"He's loving it," said Bill. "Just like me when I was a boy."

Kate smiled and nodded gently. Then Bill looked away and slowly surveyed the park once more. "You know," he said, "I understand they didn't have the same standards in those days, but for all its faults, I still miss the Big Dipper. That old roller-coaster had a lot of character, I can tell you. The way it used to rumble and roar, towering above the park. God, the whole thing was made of wood and bolts – can you believe it? And that crazy Ghost Train, with a great big skeleton sitting above the entrance. I have to say, that was actually a lot of fun too – especially if you had a girlfriend. And I remember there was another ride called the River Caves. I used to love that one. It was always cool and peaceful in there – really good in summer. Ah . . . what else was there? Oh yes – the Cha-Cha; Davy Jones Locker; the Mirror Maze. They were all really good." He shook his head a little. "They've all gone – such a pity."

Kate stared off down the concourse. "Yes, things change – it's all quite different now," she said. "Still, if you look around, they've managed to keep a lot of the old styling – the funny faces and pictures, and things like that. And you know, it's not *all* gone. A few of the old buildings and rides are the same. Look at this carousel. And see – the Rotor's over there . . . and they've still got the Wild Mouse and the Dodgems. And of course, down the far end they've still got Coney Island." She thought for a moment. "Actually, I remember the man at the counter said Coney Island is still one of the best places for young kids. So why don't we go down there next, and after that we can make our way back."

"Yes, that sounds fine," Bill agreed. "I'd love to see Coney Island again. Let's hope it hasn't changed too much."

"No Dad, I think you're going to like Coney Island."

They made their way amid the throng of visitors on the main thoroughfare, and headed towards the far end of the park. Chris had been inspired by his first ride on the carousel, and was not in the mood for dawdling. Bill, however, was pausing every now and then as he got his bearings and recollected the Luna Park of his youth.

"I think the Ghost Train was right here, and just over there was the River Caves," he said. "But I'm not quite sure – it was such a long time ago. Oh, look at that!" He pointed to a metal plaque that had been fixed to a nearby wall. "See, I was right. It's a memorial plaque to the victims of the Ghost . . ."

"Okay Dad," said Kate, quickly interrupting him. "That's fine, but let's not talk about it."

Chris had not been listening, and was focused on the massive facade of Coney Island in the distance. "Come on Granddad – let's go!" he demanded. "We've got to get to Coney Island!"

"Yes, c'mon Dad – let's go!" Kate said. She smiled and took hold of her father's hand, steering him onwards.

Chris led the way as they climbed the steep wooden staircase into the famous old funhouse. From the walkway on the upper level they could all look down into the vast interior of the building, and the entirety of Coney Island spanned out before them. While the world was constantly changing around it, this extraordinary parcel of space had remained unaltered, invariably resting as an enormous time capsule from the 1930s.

"Woh!" Chris exclaimed, wide-eyed, as he surveyed the scene. Walkways and railings moved back and forth, then rose and fell.

83

Giant wheels and barrels spun and turned. Vents expelled warm air up the pants and dresses of the unsuspecting. Vintage arcade machines lit up, rang and whistled across the floor. The constant movement of mechanisms within the structure produced a steady hum and a whirring which was mixed with the recurrent sound of children's shouting and laughter. This was regularly broken by the sudden screams of those launching themselves from the top of gigantic slides. And all was overseen by the famous, original 1930s murals and artwork adorning the walls on every side. Countless bizarre, comic figures, both human and animal, stared, gawked, peeped, winked and laughed at their funhouse guests from every angle.

"This is fantastic," said Bill. "It hasn't changed a bit. It's just as I remember. You can see – it's all exactly the same. The big slides, the Barrel of Fun, that turning-wheel thing over there, which all the kids sit on. And the old walkway with all the blowers, and that up-and-down thing over there – what's that called?"

"The Turkey Trot," said Kate.

"How'd you know that?"

"The name's written on the sign there – see."

"Oh, yeah – you're right. Well, I think it's great that they've kept it all like this." Bill turned to his grandson. "What do you think, Chris?"

"I think this is the best day of my life!" the young boy shouted.

Chris hit the floor running. He took the Joy Wheel three times, and finally muscled his way to the central point where he could sit without getting spun off. After that, he attacked the Turkey Trot with his mum till she could take no more. Then, as Kate rested a little, he and Bill climbed the tall staircase to the top of the giant slides. On his first two goes he sat in his granddad's lap and steadily gained his confidence. Kate waited at the bottom taking photos, as they hurtled down and came to rest at the padded wall, both bursting with laughter.

Chris's enthusiasm for the slides continued. Bill, however, was now tired and not prepared to climb the stairs again. So, they encouraged the boy to go solo, and he took the challenge without hesitation. They watched him dragging his mat up the huge staircase all alone – just a tiny speck of a boy on the massive wooden slope. He soon emerged from the small crowd at the top, and within seconds he was plummeting down towards them. When he got to the bottom, all he could say was "again!", and he grabbed his mat and ran to the stairs once more.

"Well, it looks like Coney Island's a winner," said Bill.

"Yes, there's no stopping him now," Kate said. Then she turned to her father. "Dad, didn't you say that the Mirror Maze was no longer here?"

"Yes, that's right. It used to be part of Davy Jones Locker, and that was all removed when they upgraded the park."

"Well, I've got news for you. Look over there." She pointed to a small area of the floor which lay to the left of the giant slides and immediately below the stairs. Being so dominated by the structures above, it seemed a little secluded, and there were very few people there.

Bill continued to peer for a second or two and, sure enough, he noted a small sign that said 'Mirror Maze'. He couldn't believe he hadn't seen it till now. "Well I'll be damned!" he said. "They moved it in here. Looks like they've set it up in the area under the slides. Can't remember what they did with that area before, but the Mirror Maze certainly wasn't there. It was outside – I remember clearly."

"So, do you want to go through the maze when Chris has had enough of the slides?"

"Absolutely. He'll love it."

They smiled briefly at the young attendant who sat at the entrance, then made their way into the maze. Chris had a basic concept of what to do, since he had already seen one maze while visiting an old

85

country estate several months earlier. That one, however, was made with large hedges, and bore little resemblance to its mirrored cousin.

He was immediately spellbound by the multitude of lights and reflections. Narrow, twisting corridors were continuously lined by dozens upon dozens of tall, gleaming mirrors, rising from floor to ceiling at every angle. Bright, fluorescent lights stood upright at the edge of each mirror. Their endless reflections resembled a forest of brilliantly illuminated tree trunks extending far into the distance. Suddenly, this luminous forest was filled in every direction with the multiple images of himself, his mother and his granddad. As the corridors turned and split, their countless reflections slipped past, they converged, they stood still, and they divided, all within the illusion of infinite space. Amidst the array of glistening mirrors to either side – from right to left and from left to right, they appeared, then disappeared, then emerged again.

"Follow me!" Chris shouted, and he forged ahead eagerly into the heart of the maze. He briefly confronted himself and a scattering of his numerous reflections at a dead end. Then he turned back and overtook his mother and grandfather again. "This way!" he said as he passed them, then veered one way and into another dead end. "No, this way!" he cried excitedly, as he overtook them once more.

"Chris, slow down – we can't keep up!" Kate called out.

"Don't worry; he can't go far," said Bill.

"But I don't want to lose him."

Bill laughed. "We won't lose him. It's not *that* complicated."

They followed on – another corner, a fork to the right, yet another dead end, then return again. Around to the left, along a way, branch to the right, then a gradual bend with an unmistakable reflection of some warm, exterior light. Just a few steps more and the exit door loomed. They burst out to be encompassed once more by the sounds of shouting and screaming in the main room.

Chris's face beamed with delight. "Mummy, that was great! I want to go again!"

"Okay, let's go again. Are you coming Dad?"

86

"Yes, I'm up for it."

Chris led the way as they walked the short distance back to the entrance. The attendant gave a customary nod as they entered for the second time.

"Follow me! I know the way!" the small boy said, as he strode ahead.

"Okay, off you go. You lead the way," said Bill, following on.

"Not too fast. We have to keep up," Kate implored.

To their great surprise, they found that Chris was right. He did know the way. His memory of the maze was excellent, and he made just one small error as he quickly led them through. Then, as they returned to the main room, Chris had only one word to say – "again!"

"Oh, no, I can't do it again," said Kate, puffing.

"Yes, that's enough for me too," said Bill. "If you want to go again, you can go by yourself. We'll wait here."

"He can't go by himself," said Kate.

"Of course he can – he's an expert. He's done it twice and it's not that hard. Go on, off you go. We'll be waiting right here when you come out."

Chris ran over to the entrance and disappeared again. As he went in, the attendant looked up briefly to check that Bill and Kate were standing by the exit. Bill raised his hand in a small gesture to confirm they were waiting.

It took less than two minutes for Chris to re-emerge.

"See – he's fine," Bill declared, as the boy came back to them.

"Mummy, I found a new way we didn't see before!" he shouted.

Kate was happy to see her son so confident. "That's good dear. Now, I think it's time to leave Coney Island and do some of the other rides outside."

"No, not yet!" Chris cried. "The mirror maze is fun! I love it!"

"But you've done it three times. Don't you want to try something else?"

"Just one more time – please! I just want to do it *one* more time."

Kate sighed and looked at Bill. He shrugged his shoulders and nodded acceptingly.

"Okay, just one more time," she said. "But this is absolutely the last one, or else we'll run out of time for the other rides – you understand?"

"Yes mum, I understand," Chris said, and he ran to the entrance and entered once more.

As Kate and Bill waited patiently, an exuberant and noisy teenage couple walked past them and entered the maze. Kate smiled affectionately at her father. "Just like you and mum all those years ago," she said.

"Pretty much," said Bill.

Then they both looked up and started to examine the strange pictures decorating the walls nearby. Several odd and curious characters, grimaced and gazed upon the floor below.

"They're weird, aren't they?" said Kate. "But I still think the old paintings are brilliant."

"Yes, you're right," said Bill. "They're part of what makes this place great. There's nothing else like them."

Another minute had passed, and Kate became a little less patient. "He seems to be taking a bit longer this time," she noted.

"Don't worry; he'll be out soon," Bill reassured her.

Just then, the teenage couple came out the exit, laughing and hugging each other.

"Excuse me, but did you see a little boy in there?" Kate asked.

"Ah . . . no, I can't remember seeing anyone in there," the young man replied, and he looked at his girlfriend. She shook her head and added, "But he may have been in one of the side corridors and we didn't see him."

"Thank you," said Kate, and she turned immediately to her father. "Dad, you know the maze better than me. Could you go through quickly and get him please? I'm worried that he's got lost in there and he'll get frightened. I'll wait here in case he comes out."

Bill wasn't worried, but he wasn't about to challenge his daughter on the issue either. "Alright," he said, "but please don't worry. I'm sure he's fine." He headed off past the attendant and went in again.

As the next couple of minutes progressed, Kate became increasingly concerned. It was a mother's instinct that made her so. She just had this niggling sense that something was wrong. As her father emerged from the exit, she immediately spoke up.

"Haven't you got him?!" she cried.

"No!" said Bill. "Didn't he come out?"

"No – not at all. Did you have a *proper* look in there?"

"Of course – absolutely! I went into every part of the maze. I swear, he's not in there."

"Well, where in the bloody hell could he be! He *must* be in there!"

"Darling, I just don't know. I'm confused about this."

"I told you he shouldn't go in there by himself! Didn't I say that?!"

"I know, I know. Kate, I'm so sorry."

The young attendant at the entrance had heard the commotion and was watching them. Kate looked over at him and called out anxiously. "Have you seen my son? Since he went in last time, he hasn't come out the exit. Did he come out through the entrance?"

"No, he didn't come out this way," the attendant shouted back. "If he hasn't come out the exit, then he must still be in there. Would you like me to go in and fetch him?"

"Yes, please do. My father couldn't find him and he must be getting scared by now."

"You stay right there – I'll get him," said the attendant. "Believe me, I know all the little places where kids get stuck!" He turned and quickly entered the maze.

Bill felt a degree of shame that he hadn't been able to find his grandson. He couldn't understand how he had missed the boy. However, when the attendant came out the exit a minute later, Bill noted a slightly perplexed look on his face.

"He's not in there," the attendant said. "He must be out here somewhere."

"But you've seen us standing here all the time," said Bill. "We've been waiting here, and we *know* he hasn't come out."

"Yes, that's right," said Kate. "He didn't come past us, so he's *got* to be in there still."

The attendant remained considerate, but shook his head slowly. "Ma'am, I know the maze really well. I know every bit of it, and I can tell you he's just not in there."

"Well, I'm sorry," Kate said, with a crackle of fear in her voice, "but maybe he's got stuck in some place you *don't* know."

The attendant looked at them worriedly for a few seconds. "Alright, I understand, I tell you what I'm going to do. I'll close off the maze right now, and I'll call my supervisor and get him down here. He'll be able to sort this out. But in the meantime, can you *please* have a good look around the room. I do feel that somehow he's managed to come out and get past you." He quickly walked back to the entrance and extended a thick barrier rope across the doorway. Then he pulled out his phone and started to make a call.

The situation was now starting to make Kate feel very unsettled. She could also see signs of tension building in her father's face.

"Dad, you stay here and keep an eye out for him. I'll search around the floor. God, if I find him out here, he's in so much trouble. But I'm stumped as to how he got past us."

"Alright," said Bill, "but please stay calm and search carefully. Take your time."

As Kate headed out across the floor, Bill started to scan the walkways above. A few minutes later, a smartly-dressed man in his forties approached the entrance to the maze and spoke directly to the attendant. Bill couldn't hear them, but realised this must be the young man's supervisor. He watched the two men closely. The supervisor crossed his arms and remained expressionless as he listened intently to what the attendant had to say. Occasionally, the two of them would glance over at Bill as he stood by the exit. After

90

a short period, the attendant turned and re-entered the maze, while the supervisor strode over to see Bill.

"Good afternoon," he said rather solemnly, as he shook Bill's hand. "My name's Ryan Cavanagh – I'm the manager of the Park."

"Bill Patterson," said Bill. "Thank you for helping us."

"I understand you've lost your grandson."

"Yes, we think so. At this stage we just don't know where he is. My daughter's gone off looking all about Coney Island, and I hope she finds him, but we don't think he came out of the maze. We were waiting for him right here, and as far as we can tell, he just didn't come out."

"Hmm," said Ryan. "Well, I've got a member of staff going through the maze again, but he told me he's already done a good search, so it's unlikely he'll find him in there. I think the chances are we'll find him playing around out here somewhere."

At that moment, Kate came running over to them, puffing deeply. "I can't find him! I've searched everywhere!"

"Oh no," whispered Bill, and he sighed despondently. "Kate, I'm so sorry; but I'm *sure* we're going to find him. This is the manager, Ryan. He's come to help us. Ryan, this is my daughter, Kate."

"Sorry we have to meet like this," said Ryan, stepping forward to shake her hand. "I understand this situation is stressful, but I agree with your father – we *are* going to find your son."

"Well, I've looked everywhere in Coney Island and I can't see him anywhere! I'm sure he's still in the maze. He went in and he didn't come out!"

"Yes, so I've been told."

"Is there *anywhere* in there where a small child could hide or be concealed?"

"No," said Ryan, shaking his head. "There are no closets, no trapdoors, no secret passageways. Only corridors, and they're all safety-checked each week." Then he thought for a moment and asked, "Did you happen to see anyone else go in there at the same time?"

"Yes," said Bill. "There was a young couple that went in just after Chris. But we saw them come out and we spoke to them. They said they hadn't seen him, and they seemed very genuine."

Just then, the young attendant came out the exit and immediately approached them. "Sir, he's absolutely not in there. I've double checked every part of the maze, and I can't see a sign of him."

"But we're *sure* he didn't come out!" cried Kate.

"Yes, this just doesn't make sense," added Bill.

"I hear what you're saying, but let's think logically about this," said Ryan, calmly. "We do know that he's definitely not in the maze, so he *must* have come out. He must be here in the main room somewhere. Was there any time – even a brief moment – when you weren't watching the exit?"

Both Kate and Bill looked at each other. Then Kate took a deep breath and wiped a tear from her eye. "We were looking up at the pictures on the walls," she admitted. "But that was only for a few seconds – maybe ten seconds at the most – and even if he did come out then, he would have come straight to us. He wouldn't go wandering off by himself. He's not like that."

"I do understand, and I feel for you, I really do," said Ryan. "But I've seen this situation before. Children can get very excited when they're in here, and sometimes they do unusual things. Let's have a proper search around the main floor. I'll get some staff to help us, and I'm sure we'll find him."

"But what if he's been abducted or something like that!" Kate said. "Maybe he's been taken out of Coney Island! We could be wasting time!" Her eyes filled with tears at the thought, and she began to gently sob. Bill placed his arm around her shoulder and hugged her tightly, his face now deeply ingrained with the stress of the situation.

"Alright . . . I understand," said Ryan. "I do appreciate your concerns – I have a small child myself. So, although I think it's highly unlikely that he's outside Coney Island, I will activate our procedure, just in case he's really missing. If you give me his name

92

and a description, I'll contact my secretary and get her to make a public address throughout the park. Also, I'll call the police and get them started." He paused for a second in thought. "Now, as for the exits," he continued, "there are a couple of smaller ones and I'll notify other staff to keep a watch at them. But Bill, what I'd like you to do, is to go down to the main exit. You know – the entrance and exit under the big smiling face. Speak to the member of staff who's there, and you can both keep a good look-out for him. My staff will contact me if you find him."

"Yes, that's a good idea," said Bill.

Kate had been thinking ahead. She had taken her phone from her bag and was scrolling through some photos. "His name is Chris and he's five years old. This is what he looks like." She moved forward and showed Ryan a photo on the screen.

"Okay – *Chris, five years old*," Ryan confirmed, while studying the photo closely. Then he turned to the young attendant and said, "Nobody's to go into the maze until this situation is sorted out – you understand?"

"Yes sir. I've already got the maze sealed off."

"Good. So, I suggest, since you already know what the boy looks like, you grab a couple more staff from the enquiry counter over there, and then you and Kate make a thorough search of the whole of Coney Island. If we don't find him after that, then at least we've got the ball rolling." He pulled his phone from his jacket pocket and glanced from Bill to Kate, and then back to the attendant. "Okay," he said, "that's the plan everyone – let's go."

As Bill headed off towards the exit, Kate and the attendant proceeded to the enquiry counter in the middle of the floor. There, Kate showed the photo to a further two female staff members, while the attendant explained the situation. From time to time they all looked over in the direction of the maze, and could see Ryan engaged in a conversation on his phone. Then they agreed to split into pairs. Kate accompanied one of the ladies to one side of the floor, while the attendant and his partner went to the other.

93

After a few minutes, they heard a somewhat crackly public address come over the speakers around the building. It gave Chris's name and a short description, and said that anyone discovering the missing boy was to take him to the management office or to the enquiry counter in Coney Island.

After about ten minutes, they all reluctantly knew that their search for little Chris was exhausted. All their efforts in looking for him and repeatedly calling his name had been futile. Kate was feeling more and more sure that her son had been abducted, and there was now a fear and a tension within her that was wrenching at her heart. As they reassembled back at the maze, they discovered the manager standing on a walkway above, staring across the room.

"We couldn't find him! Is there any word?" Kate shouted out, as she looked up at him.

"No, I'm afraid not," said Ryan, in a disheartened fashion, and he quickly made his way down the stairs and joined them at the maze entrance. "I'm so sorry," he said to Kate. "I just felt so sure that we'd find him in here."

"I can't help but think that someone must have taken him," she said. "If he's not here and he's not in the maze, that's the only thing I can think of!" Once again, her eyes filled with tears, and the lady who'd accompanied her on the search put an arm around her.

The full gravity of the situation was also beginning to show on Ryan's face. "Alright," he said, "I think we should go back to my office. The police will be arriving shortly, and we'll meet them there. I'll continue to communicate with my staff, and when the police join us, we can start a full-scale search of the park. Are you able to phone your father? I'd like to leave him at the front entrance if possible, but I understand if you want him to come back to be with you."

"Yes, I want my father with me now; but he doesn't have a mobile. Can you please get someone to bring him back?"

"Yes, of course. I'll contact the front gate and have someone bring him to the office immediately. Kate, I'm so sorry this has happened, but we're going to get to the bottom of this situation, and

I'll do everything in my power to find your boy." Ryan turned to the young attendant. "Thanks for your help. I'll get you to stay here at the maze and continue to keep an eye out."

"Yes sir," said the attendant.

"And you two," Ryan said to the other staff, "you've been very helpful, thank you. At this stage, I'll get you to resume your duties at the counter. And if you happen to hear or see anything, contact me straight away, of course."

They both nodded, and the older one, who was comforting Kate said, "I really hope you find him soon. I wish you all the best."

"Okay, come with me now," Ryan said softly, and he placed his hand on her shoulder in an attempt to console her. Then they walked in silence to the Coney Island exit.

Although Kate instinctively kept looking for her son, she spent most of the next few minutes in a dream-like haze. The reality of the situation was fully settling in, and her mind was abuzz with a mixture of confusion, fear and anger. She heard and saw very little of the park around her, and hardly felt her feet touching the ground as they made their way out of the old funhouse and down the pedestrian concourse to the administration office.

During that time, Ryan had updated the police and was told they would arrive in a few minutes. He also managed to phone the front entrance and arranged for Bill to return to them.

When they arrived outside the office, Bill came jogging down the concourse, quite out of breath. "Oh, Kate!" he said, his voice trembling as he wrapped his arms around her and pulled her in close. "Oh, my darling girl, I don't know what to say. I just can't think!" Then they stood there for several seconds; Bill's arms around her as she wept uncontrollably on his shoulder.

Ryan stood to one side, staring vacantly at the ground. When his phone rang, he pulled it from his pocket and answered the call. "Ryan," he said sombrely. He listened for a few seconds, then suddenly his eyes opened wide and he looked up at Kate and Bill, who stared back at him apprehensively. "What?!" Ryan gasped.

95

"Where?! . . . Oh, my God! . . . Yes, yes, we'll come straight back!" He finished the call, and shouted ecstatically to Kate and her father. "They found him! He's perfectly safe!"

Kate heard clearly what the manager said, but at first, she found herself unable to speak – not even a word. While she clung to her father's waist, she stared at Ryan and continued to cry. Her tears, however, were no longer born from overwhelming distress, but rather, from utter relief. It was as if her gentle heart had been dragged relentlessly in one direction, and was then arrested and flung back in the other.

"Where is he?" she asked, as she gathered herself.

"He's in Coney Island, at the maze."

"What! *Inside* the maze?" Bill asked, astounded.

"I don't think so. Apparently, they found him by the exit."

"Incredible. So, he was in there *somewhere*," said Bill. "God knows where he'd got to."

Kate wiped her eyes with her hands. "He's safe – that's all that matters. Let's go and get him." She started walking quickly back, and the two men followed at her heels.

By the time they had entered Coney Island and were striding along the upper walkway, they could all look down and see young Chris standing outside the maze below. The young attendant was with him, and so were the two women from the enquiry counter. Kate broke into a jog and hastily made her way down the stairs to the main floor.

When Chris saw his mother, he ran to her with his arms raised in the air. "Mummy!" he shouted, his face beaming with delight.

"Oh Chris, my boy – my beautiful boy!" she cried, as she scooped him up and hugged him tightly. "Where have you been?! We've been looking for you everywhere!"

"Mummy, I found some new friends!" he said excitedly.

"What friends? Where?"

"Some other boys. I was playing with some boys in the garden."

"What garden, Chris? There's no garden in here."

"Yes there is. On the other side of the maze."

Kate was confused. She put Chris down on the floor and squatted beside him. "Chris, I don't understand. You went into the maze and we didn't see you come out. Where did you go?"

"I told you. I went into the maze and then into the garden. That's where my friends are playing. They have a funny little train, and we went on lots of rides. It's so bright there, Mummy. The garden is so bright and beautiful."

"But, this *garden* – how did you get there? Did you come out of the maze to get to the garden?"

Chris gazed at his mother for a few seconds, and seemed a little puzzled. "I can't remember. I'm sorry. I just remember seeing the garden."

Kate stared back at her son with a degree of impatience, and then gave a large sigh. "I've got absolutely no idea where you got to, but wherever you were, you knew we were waiting for you. After the maze, you should have come straight back to us. You've been gone for a long time, and we've been really worried about you. Chris, you just can't go off like that. Do you understand?"

"I'm sorry Mummy, but it was so much fun, and the boys said I *have* to stay with them. They said I needed to stay, so I played with them. And we all went on the train together. But later, the dad of the two little boys said I must go, and he brought me back to the maze."

"So, there was a *man* who brought you back to the maze?"

"Yes, their dad. He showed me back to the maze."

Bill was standing next to Kate and his grandson, listening carefully. So too was Ryan and the three other employees. Like his daughter, Bill couldn't make sense of what had happened to the boy. He was just so greatly relieved that Chris was safe and well.

Ryan turned to the three staff members and spoke softly. "Did any of you *actually* see him come out of the maze?"

"No," whispered the young attendant. "I just looked around and saw him standing by the exit. He was looking a bit lost and frightened, and I immediately recognised him of course. Then I called to the others and they came running over from the counter."

"And did you ask him where he's been?"

"Yes sir; he said the same thing. He kept on saying that he was playing in a garden – playing with some boys and going on a train."

Kate looked up at Ryan. "Does this make sense to you – this garden with a train?"

Ryan nodded slowly. "Yes, I know where he was. There's only one place it could be. It's not really a *garden*, but there's a small park with a picnic area just out the back of Coney Island. And there are some rides for small children out there too – including a train. He must have come out of the maze and gone there." He frowned and thought deeply for a moment. "He can get out of Coney Island because the exit is not attended, but coming back in again would be more difficult. He couldn't do it by himself. There's only one entrance, and the staff would question a small boy who's unaccompanied. So, it must be true – this man he's talking about. He must have brought your son back in and just let him go. But it seems incredible to me that this man wouldn't help him find you. You can't account for the actions of people sometimes."

To Kate and Bill, what Ryan was saying seemed very logical, and would make perfect sense to anyone else. However, they knew the boy intimately, and they still found it difficult to believe that he would wander off and leave Coney Island without them.

"Oh well, at least we've got a good idea of what happened," said Bill, wishing to be polite and not question the manager further.

"So, would you like to go around the back to this other area and the picnic ground?" Ryan asked. "Maybe your son can point out the man and the boys he was playing with."

"No, that's not necessary," said Kate. "I don't need to see where he went or who he was with." She placed her hand on her son's head and stroked his hair. "Chris is back with us now. He's safe and well, and he seems very happy. That's all that matters. Besides, it's getting late and I'm exhausted. I just want to go home."

"Can't we go on some more rides?" Chris asked.

"Oh no," Kate answered quickly, glaring at her son for a second. "I think we've had more than our fair share of excitement for one afternoon."

"Yes, I agree," said Bill, and he picked up Chris and held him firmly.

"Alright then," said Ryan. "Well, I'm as relieved as you that the boy's been found, and if you're happy now, I think we can say this situation's been resolved. Would you allow me to call off the police?"

"Yes, certainly," said Kate.

Ryan's phone rang once more, and he took it from his pocket and studied the screen for a second. "Ah, perfect timing – it's my secretary," he said, as he glanced at Kate and Bill, and then took the call. "Diane, if you're phoning to tell me the police have arrived, I'm happy to say we don't need them anymore. The boy's been found and he's perfectly . . ."

He suddenly stopped talking, and listened intently to the call. "What?!" he said abruptly. "The police are where? . . . What happened? . . . Oh, my God!" He placed his hand against his forehead and stared at the floor. "I can't believe it! Is anyone injured? . . . Okay, stay in the office by the phones . . . and contact Stuart in Maintenance and organise the barriers. I'll be down there in two minutes."

Ryan finished the call, then looked up at Kate and Bill. All signs of the pleasure and satisfaction he had experienced just moments earlier had been wiped from his face.

"Is everything okay?" Bill asked.

"No, it's not," he said gravely. "I'm sorry, but I haven't got time to talk. There's been an incident, and I must go immediately. I'm so happy the boy's safe." He turned quickly to his staff members. "You all stay here and continue your normal operations for the moment. I can't talk about it now, but someone will contact you soon and give you an update. So, keep your radios handy." He took off rapidly towards the exit, leaving Kate, Bill and the others standing in a small group by the maze.

"Sounds a bit serious," said Kate. "Dad, I think we should go now. Are you right carrying Chris?"

"Yes, I'm fine," said Bill. "I agree – it's definitely time to go home."

Kate turned to the three staff members. "I'd like to thank you all for the help you've given us in finding my son. You've all been excellent and I really appreciate it."

"You're most welcome," said the older of the two ladies.

"I never had a kid get *that* lost before. I'm so glad we found him," said the young attendant.

"Yes, thanks again . . . we have to go," Kate said. She headed off with Bill and her son towards the Coney Island exit, while the three employees returned to their work.

Before they went through the exit turnstile, Bill looked about and surveyed the old funhouse one last time. He took a slow, deep breath and filled his lungs with the scent of the room. The continuous movement and sound of the rides, the murals and artwork, the laughter and screams of the children – constants for over eighty years, he thought to himself. He realised there was now a very real chance he would never return.

He smiled gently at his grandson, who sat peacefully in his arms. The small boy looked back inquisitively and gave his grandfather a big hug.

"Granddad," he said, "what's an *incident*?"

They made their way out of Coney Island and headed towards the main exit at the front of the park. It was now late afternoon and the warm sunlight cast long shadows across the pedestrian concourse. The park was still in full motion, and they could hear the persistent whirring and bumping of the Dodgems to their left, and the rumble and screams from the Wild Mouse above. Yet, something was different. The people on the concourse were not moving in the usual way. Many were standing still and gazing toward the top end of the park.

Kate and Bill stopped and followed their gaze. In the middle distance, the giant Ferris wheel formed a sharp silhouette against a bright, golden sky. However, it was immediately obvious that the perfect symmetry of the wheel had been broken. Something was alarmingly wrong with one of the cabins. Although still attached to the wheel, it had collapsed and was askew, dangling well out of its normal position.

Bill had his teeth clenched and was grimacing at the sight before them. "Oh . . . that doesn't look good," he whispered.

"No . . . it doesn't," Kate agreed. "Now we know where Ryan's gone."

Chris had been resting his head on Bill's shoulder. "What are you talking about?" he asked.

"Nothing for you to worry about," said Kate, calmly. "Come on – let's keep walking."

"Can't we go on just one more ride?"

"No, I'm afraid not Chris. It's getting late and definitely time for us to go."

The boy's face looked a little glum. He rested his head once more upon Bill's shoulder and took consolation in the comfort of being carried.

As they continued towards the main exit, a female voice came over the speakers about the park delivering a loud public address. "Ladies and gentlemen and children – it is with great regret that, due to unforeseen circumstances, Luna Park will be closing shortly to all members of the public. Please follow the directions of staff and proceed to your nearest exit. Also, please keep your passes, which may be used again in the future. The management and staff of Luna Park sincerely apologise for any inconvenience this may cause."

"What are they saying, Mummy?"

"Oh . . . they're just saying that it's closing time and unfortunately everyone has to leave."

101

They kept walking and joined a large number of people who were heading in the same direction. While the focus of conversations around them was the event in the air, Bill and Kate refrained from talking because they didn't want to alarm the boy. He still hadn't noticed the wheel, and didn't appreciate what was happening.

They soon met a park employee who was directing everyone to the left side of the concourse in order to avoid the area around the base of the Ferris wheel. There they could see another small group of employees in overalls that were taking wooden barriers from a utility van and erecting them in a wide arc over the concourse. A police car with its lights flashing was parked nearby, and another police vehicle was just arriving.

As they approached the carousel, Bill and Kate looked up again and were able to gain a clearer view of the problem. Each of the Ferris wheel cabins was supported by a pair of massive struts, or 'spokes', extending outwards from a central hub. One outer section of a spoke carrying the disabled cabin had fractured, and this had caused the spoke to bend significantly. The supporting braces above the cabin had also buckled and snapped. Although still connected to the spoke, the cabin had fallen at least two metres and was now suspended precariously near the roof of its neighbour. Many of the other cabins still had people on board who were looking out anxiously across the park and towards the ground. Bill and Kate couldn't see any passengers in the fallen cabin, but since it was still so high above the ground, it was impossible to be sure.

The wheel was turning very slowly, and as each cabin arrived at the loading platform, some park employees and a couple of police officers were assisting passengers to get out and move away from the area. Bill could just see an ambulance edging its way slowly through the crowd at the main exit.

Chris was starting to feel a little tired and was staring vaguely through the mass of people about him. Then, from the corner of his eye he saw a nearby flash of colour that he recognised instantly. His face lit up and he called out excitedly. "Look Granddad – that's the clown we met before! Hi clown! Hi clown!" he shouted, as he waved. His sharp little voice cut through the general hum and chatter of the crowd. The clown had just finished talking to another couple, and he turned immediately and walked over to meet them. As he approached, he gave Chris a smile, but even his thick makeup couldn't hide an underlying feeling of unease.

Bill leaned forward and whispered subtly in the clown's ear. "He doesn't know."

The clown glanced at Bill and Kate, then gave an almost imperceptible nod of his head. "Hello, my little friend. How was your day?" he said cheerfully.

"It was great! Do you have to go home too?" Chris asked.

"Oh . . . yes. We all have to go home now. But I do hope you can come back soon."

"Yes – I want to!"

The clown gave another big smile. "Well, you know you're always welcome."

"Dad, do you mind going ahead for a moment?" Kate said. "I just want to chat to the clown for a second."

"Yes, that's fine," said Bill, and he continued to walk ahead slowly with Chris in his arms.

"Bye-bye clown! Bye!" Chris shouted, as he was carried away.

The clown smiled broadly again and waved farewell to the boy. Then he turned to Kate.

"Oh, this is terrible," she said. "We were just speaking to your manager, Ryan, down at Coney Island when this happened. Has anyone been injured?"

"Well, it's an absolute miracle," the clown said. "Virtually all of the cabins had people in them, but that cabin, thank God, is empty. Can you believe it?!"

"Oh, my goodness – that *is* very lucky. Well, I do hope you manage to get all the people away safely. Thankyou – I won't take up any more of your time."

103

"You're most welcome. I do hope you're able to come back soon." And, as the clown waved goodbye, for the first time his face looked a little sad.

Kate moved off and met up again with her father and son, who were waiting nearby. As the crowd moved slowly forward, Chris continued to rest his head comfortably on his grandfather's shoulder. Within a minute they were moving through the main exit under the big smiling face.

Just outside, a large fire brigade rescue vehicle with its beacons flashing had parked by the edge of the harbour. Another ambulance was arriving, and some police officers were addressing the cameras of the news crews that had arrived at the scene.

"Is there a fire?" Chris asked.

"No darling. They're just down here to look at the beautiful harbour."

Against the warm glow of the western sky, the young boy thought it all looked very exciting. As they continued to walk away from the park, Chris kept his eyes on the bright smiling face. It didn't seem to look so big and scary anymore. It just got smaller and smaller, and finally disappeared from sight.

The sun had slipped below the horizon, and the heavily lit buildings of the city were gradually developing a stark contrast to the deepening night sky. As their car crossed the Harbour Bridge, Kate and Bill sat in the front, quietly reflecting on the events of the day. Chris sat warm and cosy in the rear, listening to the hum of the engine, and fascinated by the smooth procession of bright city lights.

The silence was broken by Bill. "We were planning to go on the Ferris wheel, weren't we?" he said softly.

There was a further moment of silence.

"Yes, we were," said Kate.

"But we got held up in Coney Island."

"Yes . . . we did."

They resumed their period of thoughtful silence as the car continued on the expressway, moving steadily past the city and into the suburbs. After a while, Bill looked back at his grandson and smiled warmly. "How are you going, Chris?"

"Good," the boy replied, in a simple and upbeat manner.

"Did you have fun today?"

"It was the best day ever, Granddad."

"What was your favourite thing?"

Chris thought for a moment, then said, "The mirror maze."

"Yes, I thought you might say that."

"The mirror maze . . . and the garden."

"The garden too?"

"Yes Granddad – playing in the garden was *really* good."

Bill turned back to the front seat and whispered in his daughter's ear. "He doesn't seem to be affected by anything."

Kate nodded and continued to concentrate on the road.

"Granddad, look what I got," said Chris.

Bill turned around again and saw Chris pulling something from the pocket of his pants. "What's that?" he asked.

"It's something the boys gave me."

"Oh really – can I have a look?"

"You can have a look Granddad, but I want it back – it's mine."

"Yes, of course," said Bill. He reached back and Chris handed him a small roll of paper. Bill turned on the interior light and put on his reading glasses. He studied the item for several seconds without saying a word. It lay peacefully in his hand while something stirred deep in his memory. A small roll of bright yellow coupons, each embossed with the image of a smiling face and the words 'Luna Park'.

"What is it?" Kate asked.

"Well . . . they're *tickets*," said Bill, a little bewildered. "These are just like the old tickets we had when I was a kid. I thought you said they don't use them anymore."

"They don't," said Kate, shaking her head.

105

Bill turned again to the back seat. "Where did you get these, Chris?"

"I told you Granddad – the boys gave them to me."

"The boys?"

"Yes Granddad. The boys in the garden – they gave them to me. They said they didn't need them anymore."

* * * * * * * * * * *

The Cup

The ancient abbey lies in ruins on a hilltop overlooking the small coastal town. From its broken walls, one gains a clear view of most of the town's old stone buildings, its irregular network of narrow streets, and its cosy and colourful boat harbour. One may also look far out to sea. There, a tall ship under full sail passes slowly by, just like the thousands of others that have graced these shores over the centuries.

It is late morning on a warm summer's day. The sun is shining brightly, there's not a cloud in the sky, and a light breeze caresses the remnants of the old church. The grounds are filled with hundreds of lively people carrying a vast array of old wares, antiques and artefacts. They swarm and pulse about the ruin like an army of bees around a hive.

A smartly-dressed woman in her early forties stands outside the abbey walls and presents herself to a small video production crew. A makeup artist makes some final adjustments to her jacket and hair. The director makes some short remarks and then she addresses the camera with a broad smile.

"A very big welcome to The Antiques Show. This is our first episode for the year 2000, and we're coming to you today from the ruins of Whitby Abbey in North Yorkshire. There has been a monastery here since the 7th Century, and then a Benedictine Abbey was built about 1100. The Gothic church you see behind me was built in the 13th Century, however it was disestablished during the Suppression of the Monasteries under Henry the 8th. Since that time, the shell of the church has fallen further and further into ruin, exposed as it is to the action of the elements. In such a setting, who knows what sort of treasures we may find? And on this beautiful, sunny day, as you can see, many hundreds of locals have come out to share their possessions with us." She clasps her hands together and offers another big smile to the camera.

In the shadow of the nave, a large crowd of people have gathered around an elderly, grey-haired gentleman, wearing an old sports jacket and large, horn-rimmed spectacles. He is Professor Ian St. Clair, a highly respected expert in antiquities, and he stands next to a younger, thick-set man in his thirties, who is accompanied by his six-year-old daughter. The girl is carefully holding a dark-brown-coloured, stone cup. A second camera and sound crew move in to get a tight shot of the three of them. The professor begins to speak in a mature and perfectly composed Oxford accent.

"I'm always delighted when I see parents bringing their children along. It's great to see the younger ones so involved in antiques, and the items they bring in are often very interesting and sometimes amusing. When I first glanced at your daughter, I said to myself, 'Oh that's nice – she's brought an old cup', but then there was something about the cup itself that grabbed my attention. Before I continue, do you mind if I hold it?"

The professor holds out his hand gently towards the young girl. She looks up a little apprehensively and clutches the cup with both hands close to her chest.

"Lucy, it's okay," says the father, as he bends down to the girl. "The man just wants to hold it so he can talk to us about it." He looks back at the professor with a tentative smile. "I'm sorry. She was a little nervous about coming here today. Kept on saying the cup is very special. I'm not so sure. Seems to me it's just an old piece of bric-a-brac. But she thinks it's precious, so I thought we may as well find out." He turns back to his daughter. "Come on darling. Let's give the man the cup. He's the one to tell us about it."

The girl hesitates for a second, but then takes a deep breath and slowly gives the cup to the professor. He cradles it gently in both hands and holds it up close to his face, studying it carefully with a look of calm intrigue.

"Firstly, may I ask, from where did you get this cup?"

"Well, we went to the flea market here in Whitby about two weeks ago," replies the father. "I'm always after a bargain, and my daughter was keen to buy something too – you know, just for fun. So, I gave her a pound and said go off and buy anything you want. Then, a few minutes later she came back with this cup."

"And did she say who sold it to her?"

"Umm, I think she said she got it from an old lady." The father looks down at his little girl. "Lucy, is that right?"

"Yes . . . an old lady," says the girl.

"And it cost you *one* pound?" confirms the professor.

"Yes," says the father, nodding. "She didn't have any change, so it was one pound."

"Hmm," says the professor, shaking his head slightly, with a hint of a smile. "And do you know anything about the cup?"

"Not a thing," replies the father, "but it looks a bit old. I think it's made of marble . . . and it's got an interesting pattern on it."

"I think it's beautiful," whispers the girl.

"I couldn't have put it better myself," says the professor. "Although very simple, it is indeed a work of beauty." He raises the cup again, so all in the crowd may see it. The cameraman zooms in, and the professor continues. "The first thing I noticed about this cup was the shape. You see this rounded shape – like half a sphere, with a small footed base. It's typical of cups used in ancient times. It's straightforward, uncomplicated, relatively easy to make. Cups of this shape could be made of metal, or stone, or clay – sometimes even from wood. However, this one's quite exceptional. It's not made of marble, but actually a very fine-grained, precious stone called agate. And most interestingly, this particular type of agate, with this specific colour and texture, is quite unique to the region of ancient Palestine.

I believe it's between two and two-and-a-half thousand years old, and in those days, it would only have been used for ceremonies and special occasions."

A murmur rises from the crowd.

For a moment, the girl's father remains silent and gazes vacantly at the cup with his mouth slightly open. "So, you're saying this is a real treasure," he says slowly. "You actually think my daughter is right – that it's *special*."

"Yes, I believe so," says the professor. "But there's more I have to say."

The crowd falls into silence once more.

"You see these markings here – carved around the outer rim of the cup." He turns the cup slowly in his hand and points to the markings. "Well, that's not a *pattern*, as you referred to it earlier. It is in fact a form of writing – *Aramaic* to be exact. All these lines and squiggles are actually names written in Aramaic script. And the most amazing thing is that these names, written right here, are the names of the twelve apostles. Look, this one is 'Peter' . . . and that's 'Andrew', 'James', 'John', 'Philip', 'Thomas', 'Simon'. This one is 'Matthew'. This one is 'Thaddaeus', 'Bartholomew' . . . and this one here is 'Judas'.

The crowd begins to buzz again.

"Now, if we're really lucky," continues the professor, "we may find one more name on this cup." He looks intently, all around the outside of the cup, then turns it upside-down. "Ah, here it is, neatly carved into the base. This is the name 'Jesus'. You see, Aramaic was the language of Jesus and his disciples."

"I'm not sure I understand," says the father. "What exactly is this cup?"

"Well, to put it simply," says the professor, calmly peering over the top of his horn-rims, "I think you and your daughter have acquired the Holy Chalice – that is, the cup used by Jesus and his twelve chosen disciples at the Last Supper. According to various writings,

Jesus gave thanks, broke bread, and then they all shared wine from this cup."

"So, you think this is the *Holy Grail?!*" splutters the father.

The professor frowns a little. "Some people have referred to it by that name, but with such a title, the cup used at the Last Supper starts getting muddled up with all sorts of romantic stories about the blood of Christ and knights on quests, and so on – stories that have no real foundation. I prefer to say the 'Holy Chalice', but we can call it the 'Grail' if you wish."

"Oh, my God!" exclaims the father, glancing briefly at his daughter. "So, what should we do with it now?"

"Well, if you wish, you're entitled to keep it; but that does pose certain risks. This is not the sort of item one should keep in the cupboard at home. It would force you to completely re-evaluate your home and contents insurance, and you may need to update your alarm system. So, it would probably be wiser to keep it in a bank. Alternatively, a safer move would be to simply give it away to a museum. I've little doubt that any of the larger and respected museums would gladly accept an item such as this." The professor pauses for a moment and takes a deep breath. "Or, of course, you could *sell* it. Now, if you do decide to put this item on the market, please don't attempt to sell it on eBay. Needless to say, 'Holy Grails' are extremely rare and highly sought after. There are a lot of people, organisations, and even governments around the world that would like to get their hands on this. So, I would recommend a specialist auction at one of the major international auction houses."

The father is staring at the professor, and seems a little bewildered.

"Now, I'm sure you're curious as to the value," says the professor. "Well, I am rather confident you could make a healthy profit on your outlay. If this cup was presented at such an auction, I would expect it to realize, conservatively, somewhere between one hundred and two hundred million pounds."

A collective "Ooooh" comes from the crowd.

The young girl has been waiting patiently by her father's side as she listens to the conversation. She looks up at her father and gently pulls at his shirt sleeve. He snaps out of his daze and looks down at her.

"Daddy," she says, "can I still use the cup for my chocolate milk?"

"Ah . . ." he replies hesitantly. "I'm not sure, darling. We'll have to think about it."

A small smile can be seen on the face of the professor. "So, there you have it," he says, carefully handing the cup back to the girl's father. "Congratulations – that's quite a find. I wish I'd gone to that flea market. Before you leave today, I do suggest you phone the local police and arrange an escort for your return home. And for God's sake – don't drop it!" He turns and looks about in the crowd for a moment. "Now, our presenter doesn't seem to be here yet, but I'm sure she'll arrive very shortly, and no doubt she'll be keen to line us up for an exclusive interview."

"Hold on a second," the father says, raising his gaze from the cup back to the professor. "Surely, you can't be serious. You're pulling my leg, right? I'm sorry, but as much as I'd like to, I just can't believe what you're saying. This may be an old cup, but we couldn't pick up the *'Holy Grail'* at a lowly flea market here in Whitby. Besides, I'm sure they've already got the Grail somewhere. Didn't I hear they have it in some church in Spain?"

The professor sighs gently and gazes up at the sky for a moment.

"Yes, yes; there is a very similar chalice in Valencia," he says, with a slight tone of impatience. "But there have always been questions about its authenticity. I think we have the *real* Holy Chalice right here. It will need to be scientifically examined, of course, but I'm very confident that such an examination will confirm this cup as the genuine one."

"Nonsense!" exclaims the father. "No one can be sure if this is the real Holy Grail. It could have come from anywhere. Probably made in China last year, for all we know."

112

"Sir," says the professor, straight-faced, while calmly crossing his arms, "I'm beginning to suspect a small degree of doubt regarding my expert evaluation."

"You bet I've got doubt. How could anyone *prove* it's genuine – even if it is thousands of years old and covered in ancient squiggles? It's probably just another old cup, and in the end, it'll give me a heap of trouble for very little reward."

The professor glares at the girl's father for a second, and then a small smile returns to his face. "Well, there is one way to prove it, beyond *any* doubt," he declares.

"And what's that?"

"It is written in the ancient manuscripts that only from one 'truly innocent and pure of heart' may the Holy Chalice be returned to God. And, as I look about here today, I believe your daughter may just be the ideal candidate."

"So, what are you proposing?"

"I propose we offer the cup to God. If God takes the cup, then we know that it is truly genuine, and if God does not take it, then we know that I am mistaken."

"And, what exactly does my girl have to do?"

"Quite simple. She just holds the cup above her head, as high as she can, and then she says the words, 'The Holy Chalice – I return to God.'"

"And what happens then – if anything does happen, of course?"

"I have absolutely no idea," admits the professor. "No one truly innocent and pure of heart has ever tried to return the Chalice to God before."

The word has spread quickly through the grounds that something special is going on, and many more people are hastily joining the crowd. The Antiques Show director and presenter have also heard the news, and have just arrived with another camera and sound crew.

The father has been staring intently at the cup for several seconds as he weighs up the proposition. "Okay," he says abruptly, "let's see if God wants the cup!" He squats down next to his daughter and carefully gives her the cup. "Here it is darling. Now, just like the man said, hold it up above your head and we'll say the words."

"But, daddy, it's a bit scary!"

"Lucy, I promise, there's absolutely nothing to worry about. Nothing's going to happen. Trust me."

"Okay daddy, I'll trust you," she says nervously, and slowly raises the cup above her head. "What do I say, daddy?"

The father glances back at the professor for a second, and then to his daughter. "Say after me," he whispers. "The Holy Chalice – I return to God."

The girl hesitates for a moment, and then slowly whispers, "The Holy Chalice . . . I return to God."

"She must say the words loudly," says the professor. "And keep the Chalice high."

"Say it loudly, darling," says the father calmly, and he motions for her to hold the cup a little higher.

The girl holds the cup as high as she can and calls out the words, "THE HOLY CHALICE – I RETURN TO GOD!"

Complete silence descends over the gathering. All eyes had been focusing on the little girl and the Chalice, but now the people in the crowd are starting to look about in all directions – over the grounds, around the ruin, out to sea, and up in the air. The professor, too, is looking about with his eyes directed more to the sky. Then he quickly looks back at the girl, who is slowly lowering the cup as she begins to tire.

"Please, keep the Chalice raised," he says, and the girl's father quickly helps to support her bending arms.

Suddenly a woman in the crowd shouts, "Look, up there!" and she points directly to the sky above. Everyone looks up. High above them – way up high in the centre of the deep blue sky, a small dark cloud can just be seen in the distance. It seems to be moving strangely, and it gradually evolves and expands. Then it turns and twists, and begins to spiral slowly downwards. Everyone suddenly realizes that it is descending towards the earth. Some people start to run off across the fields. Some embrace in fear. Some start to pray, but most just stand and gaze in awe. As it gets closer, the texture of the cloud is changing. It no longer seems like a cloud, but rather, some kind of airborne stream composed of thousands of tiny black fragments, all spinning and soaring towards them with increasing speed. A distant rumbling sound can be heard, which steadily increases, and the light breeze picks up to a gust across the grounds. Some cries and shrieks emanate from the crowd, and in the next moment the air is filled with a multitude of large black birds, several thousand in number, all swirling and fluttering chaotically about the walls of the ruined abbey.

The entire crowd is motionless; everyone staring at the spectacle above. Amidst the sound of thousands of flapping wings, the director can be heard yelling instructions to the cameramen. The girl's father, who has been watching in astonishment, now looks earnestly at the professor. "What's happening?" he cries.

"They're ravens!" shouts the professor with delight, and he raises his hands welcomingly to the sky.

"Are we in any danger?"

"No, I don't think so. Ravens are swift and strong, and one of God's most intelligent creatures. To me, it makes perfect sense that they're here."

"But what are they doing?"

"I'm not entirely sure," says the professor, "but no doubt it's something to do with that cup. Oh, look!" He points to the young girl.

The father turns to his daughter and notices her arms are now stretched out fully, and she is standing on her toes. "Lucy, are you still okay lifting the cup?!" he asks.

"Daddy, I'm *not* lifting the cup," she says anxiously. "The cup is lifting me!"

The Chalice rises to about three metres off the ground, with the girl still holding firmly and screaming as she dangles below it. Several members of the crowd gasp and cry out in shock.

"Lucy!" shouts the father. "Let go of the cup! Let go!" He lunges forward and just manages to grasp one of her ankles.

"Daddy, I can't let go! I just can't let go!" she cries frantically.

The father pulls down heavily on his daughter's ankle. Her body becomes taut, as her hands stay fixed to the cup which remains completely static in the air.

"Daddy! Stop pulling! You're hurting me!" she screams.

"It's no good," shouts the professor. "The cup lies between your daughter and the hands of God."

"But what does God want with my daughter?" cries the distraught father.

"It's not a case of God wanting your daughter," says the professor. "It's more a case of your daughter still wanting the cup! In her heart, she has to let it go."

Every person in the crowd has had their eyes fixed on the plight of the girl and the Holy Chalice. The director has been struggling to keep his cameramen focused, while the show's presenter has been trying to find the words to sum up the events. Above them all, the myriad of ravens has continued to soar and swoop about the ancient walls of the abbey.

Now, a single raven glides down gracefully and rests on the rim of the Chalice. Its presence is imposing. It is very large and perfect in stature; its feathers are pure black and glossy; its eyes golden and bright. For a moment it stands completely still and slowly surveys the silent mass of stunned onlookers. Then it leans forward and carefully looks down at the frightened young girl below. It lets out a small succession of deep croaking sounds and gently brushes her fingers with its beak.

"Lucy, the cup's not ours anymore!" the father calls out. "It was never ours. We have to give it back. Please, say goodbye and let it go!"

The girl gazes down at her father, and a look of serenity comes across her face. "Can't we keep it daddy?" she asks.

"No darling, we can't keep it."

116

"But I love it so much."

"I know you do darling, but it belongs to someone else. Sometimes we have to give away the things we love."

The girl smiles tenderly at her father. "I understand daddy," she whispers, and with that she is released and falls into his waiting arms.

The raven immediately takes off with the cup and circles once above the abbey ruins. As it does so, its companions in their multitude, swiftly unite behind it and reform the aerial stream. They build up tremendous speed as they circle once more, then turn and rise sharply, ascending towards the heavens. As they disappear from sight, a loud and deep booming sound emanates from high overhead and echoes throughout the district.

The crowd remains speechless, and all eyes move from the skies back to the professor. "Well, I think it's safe to assume that *was* the genuine Chalice," he says.

"Yes," says the father, somewhat dazed and continuing to embrace his daughter. "I'm sorry . . . I should have trusted you."

The professor chuckles to himself, and once again peers over the top of his horn-rims. "Well, I have a small admission to make," he declares. "My reputation has always rested on the integrity of my evaluations. However, I have to admit, on this occasion I wasn't totally sure. It was, perhaps, fifty-fifty at best. But then I thought – we'll never get a better chance to see if God can be revealed."

The father looks up towards the sky and takes a deep, calming breath.

"But I'll say this also," continues the professor. "You may have given away the Holy Chalice, but I truly believe you've kept your most precious possession."

The girl cuddles her father tightly. "Can we go home now, daddy?"

He nods in agreement. "Yes Lucy; let's go home."

The presenter, who has been waiting to one side, quickly moves forward to interview the father. "I appreciate this has been a shocking

117

experience for you and your daughter, as it has for all of us, but are you able to give us your feelings at this time?"

The father takes a few seconds to gather his thoughts. "Yes. Although I can hardly believe what just happened, I know it's for the best. It's not right for any one person to keep The Grail, so I don't feel that I've lost anything. We've just given it back to its owner. My daughter and I had the privilege of holding it for a short time, and that's something very special that can never be taken from us. I have no regrets. I have all that I need – I don't need any more."

The presenter turns to the professor. "And, your thoughts Professor?"

"Well, I agree with him wholeheartedly. There are some things in this world that should not be bought or sold. Some things should not even be in a museum. They need to go back to where they came from. They need to be left where they belong. That's all I have to say."

The father gives a small smile to the professor, and heads off slowly. As he carries his daughter through the crowd, he whispers in her ear. "Not a word of this to your mother – you understand?"

The girl whispers back. "Yes . . . I understand. And if I ever find another cup like that one, I won't be telling *you* either."

The professor puts on his hat, collects his briefcase, and calls to the director. "I think I'm done for the day, Stan. I'm going back to the hotel. There are a couple of articles I need to work on." He starts to walk away, and the crowd silently parts to let him through.

"Thanks Ian," says the director. "Brilliant work mate – I'll see you later." He turns to the presenter. "Nancy, do you want to finish and head back to the editing room?"

"Yes," she replies. "I think I need a good glass of wine." She moves forward and composes herself once more before the camera. She runs her fingers through her hair, straightens her jacket and smiles broadly. "Well, that's something you don't see every day on the Antiques Show. What a spectacular and somewhat unexpected

118

start to the season. It certainly has been a day of fascinating revelations. Till next time. Bye-bye."

As the crowd slowly begins to disperse, the professor is making his way across the open grounds. He can hear the sound of several sirens in the distance, and notices that a small number of police cars have already entered the car park. He stops and looks back towards the ruin, as he realises the video will never see the light of day.

It is late morning on a warm summer's day. The sun is shining brightly, there's not a cloud in the sky, and a light breeze caresses the remnants of the old church.

* * * * * * * * * * * *

The Castle at Nightfall

Part 1 – The Visitors

Winter came gracefully to the Bavarian lowlands, and the first snows of the season had fallen gently upon the quiet rural landscape. Around them, wooden farm houses, barns and the occasional village, dotted a countryside caressed by a pristine white veil. The small road they were driving on had been cleared that morning, and the snow piled thick upon its edges. It ran like a dusky waving ribbon between the vast, frozen fields. At points on the horizon, the jagged forest brushed the fringes of a pale blue sky.

As their car passed the top of a small rise, the scene before them grabbed the attention of the young man sitting in the front passenger seat. "Can you stop the car?" he asked.

His friend in the driver's seat paid little attention and the car continued.

"Stop the car, will you! I want to take a photograph."

The driver pulled the car over abruptly and let out a large sigh. "We're never going to make Munich at this rate," he said. "I don't know why you wanted to leave the autobahn. We've still got a hundred kilometres to go, and we could have been there by now."

"Look at this – it's beautiful," the passenger replied. "You must want a photo of this. This is why we came to Europe – this is what we came to see. Not some damn autobahn. You can't see anything on an autobahn."

He took his camera from the glove box and got out of the car. The cold air smacked his face, and he braced himself against the chill.

As he walked a short distance away, he thought of the coat he had left on the back seat, but assured himself he would only be a minute.

A small number of trees stood at intervals by the road's edge; their thin branches bare of leaves but glazed in a thick white frost. Partially back-lit by the afternoon sun, the trees threw a scattering of blue-grey shadows across the foreground. To the right of the road, a perfectly smooth field of virgin snow extended to the line of the distant forest and hills. In the middle distance, a thin layer of mist rested peacefully over the field and masked the base of an old and solitary parish church. A well-ordered cemetery extended to one side, and several of its taller headstones and memorials could be seen peeking above the haze. The church's onion-domed tower stood twice the height of its nave, and soared upwards, pointing to the heavens.

David absorbed the view for a moment, before taking his photograph. This was something he would keep for his lifetime, he thought. As he turned back to the car, he noticed his friend Jason had remained in the warmth of the driver's seat but was peering intently through the window.

"Aren't you glad we left the autobahn now?" David said, as he reached for his seatbelt. "This is what I wanted. Who cares if we don't make Munich? I'm sure there'll be a hotel in the next town. You want me to do some driving?"

"No, I'm okay," Jason replied, ". . . and you're right – it's a good photo." He put the car into gear and headed off.

They had been touring Europe in a small Citroen for the past six weeks. Since collecting the car in Paris, they had travelled with few plans and stayed at hostels and cheap hotels they found along the way. Being in each-other's pockets had tested the friendship on more than one occasion, however, for the most part their objectives remained similar, and the bond they had since childhood endured.

After a few minutes, they entered a small town situated near the edge of a large forest. A quaint old guesthouse overlooked the town

122

square, but despite persistent knocking, no one answered its locked door.

"Close for vinter," said an old man in the grocery store. "Better going Munich."

As they left the town, the road ran along the fringe of the forest for several kilometres. It was the strong contrast between the bright open fields on one side, and the darkness of the forest on the other, that almost made them miss the sign. They both just caught a glimpse of it as they rushed past.

"Hey, stop, back up!" said David. "There was a sign there."

"Yeah, I saw it too," said Jason. He brought the car to a stop, and put it in reverse.

It was a simple wooden sign, stuck on a small post by the edge of the roadway. Although their German was poor, it wasn't hard to translate. "Bed and all meals, in the castle, 500 metres". An arrow pointed down a small dirt sideroad that headed deep into the forest. The young men smiled at each other and hoped the accommodation on offer would not be too much for their modest budget.

Soon, they drove past the remains of an old stone wall and entered the castle grounds. The road passed a small, frozen lake, then turned and ran across an immense clearing. In the distance, between the far side of the clearing and the surrounding forest, the young travellers had their first view of the castle. They stared in silence as it sat majestically upon a sea of pure white snow; its smooth, stone walls painted by the soft glow of wintery, afternoon light.

"Now, *this* is the sort of place I've been looking for!" said David.

"Yeah," said Jason. "As long as we can afford it."

Although extensively renovated during the seventeen-hundreds, the castle originally dated back to the late fourteenth century. It was a good example of those rather substantial and semi-ornate residences still maintained by the Bavarian nobility. Its solid walls stood three storeys high, and it held a further two levels of attic space below a massive peaked roof. The large entrance door was beautifully crafted from a splendid, burgundy-coloured hardwood.

They had already visited a number of well-known palaces and castles on their tour, and they had all been larger and quite crowded. So, to stumble upon this smaller and somewhat hidden one, away from the main tourist trails, made the experience feel unique and very personal. Although hard to define, there was something about the shape of the castle and the entrance door that intrigued David in particular.

Hans was a chef, and his wife Eva, a business woman. They recently began to rent part of the castle from the Baroness, who resided in a large apartment on the first floor. In the near future, they intended to open a fine new restaurant on the ground floor, and were delighted to meet the young travellers, who would now be the first visitors to stay in their formal guest room.

David and Jason were pleased to find that their hosts not only spoke excellent English, but were also willing to offer a generous deal. For a reasonable rate, their stay would include a private dinner with their hosts and access to the cellar, which held a large quantity of wine and locally produced beer. All this, and staying in a genuine s*chloss*. The young men were thrilled and couldn't believe their luck.

Hans showed them to their room at the far end of the ground floor. It was, without doubt, the best they had been offered all trip. There was a variety of antique paintings and ornaments on the walls, a decorative ceiling, deep window recesses, and an excellent view of the garden. The most striking feature, however, was a large double bed, which seemed as old as the castle itself. It had an enormous, dark-wooden frame, adorned with intricate carvings of scenes from the forest: fir trees, lakes, waterfalls, hunters and wild animals. Its bulky, timeworn mattress had a well-defined impression of all the persons that had lain there for several hundred years. Folded neatly at the end of the mattress was an antique quilt, made from a faded medieval tapestry, and the whole arrangement stood so high off the floor that a large wooden step had been provided.

"I'm sure you'll find this room comfortable, but the bed is very old," said Hans. "I think it's big enough but are you both happy to sleep in it?"

"I'm sorry," said Jason, "but I don't think I'd sleep well on that mattress."

"Yes, I understand. You're not accustomed to such things. We also have a small portable bed I can set up, if you wish."

"Yes, please. I'd prefer that."

David had been closely studying the carvings on the bed frame. He lay down for a moment and allowed his body to be cradled by the mattress. "Well, for me, this feels perfect. I'd love to sleep here," he declared.

"That's settled then," said Hans. "I will get the portable bed for you, Jason." He paused for a second, then smiled. "Now, I suspect you may wish to make a tour of the castle, and you're very welcome to do so, but there are a few things to remember. Please do not enter the Baroness's private apartment on the first floor. Also, should you venture into the attic, feel free to have a look, but don't touch anything. All the things in the attic belong to the Baroness, and she wouldn't forgive me if something is damaged. And please be very careful because there is no lighting installed up there."

With the sound of rapid footsteps striking creaky floorboards, they flew up the giant wooden staircase to see the attic before the daylight failed. The stair finished at a landing, and there stood a large unpainted door, nicked and cut over the years by the passage of countless bulky items. As they opened it and stepped inside, the air became cool and saturated with the rich scents of antique wood and old fabrics. Scattered along the sides of the room were numerous items, all softly lit by the filtered afternoon light from a few small windows at the far end. The entire space was completely still, and seemed suspended in time, waiting patiently for the day when it would breathe new life.

"God, will you look at all this stuff!" said Jason.

"Now, this is the sort of attic I'd *expect* to see in an old castle," said David.

The young men wandered about and discovered many fascinating old things. There was a rich assortment of antique furniture, clocks and musical instruments. Also, traditional clothing, old books, paintings, stuffed animals, and a good selection of vintage dolls and children's toys. To their frustration, they found they couldn't access everything, and could only guess what lay hidden inside several large wooden chests.

At the far end of the floor, within a massive glass cabinet, were two suits of armour, some swords, shields, lances, and various other items of old weaponry. While Jason sized himself against the armour, David was more interested in the swords.

"The Baroness sure had some cool ancestors," said Jason. "Do you think if we asked real nicely, she'd let us dress up for dinner?"

"Ha! We can only wish," David replied. "But you go ahead and ask her if you want. If she lets you try it on at dinner time, for God's sake don't eat too much."

"You wouldn't want to drink much either. Must have been bloody hard to pee."

As they moved on and made their way around the other side of the cabinet, they found a somewhat hidden and dusty set of steps that led up to the attic's second level. This was a smaller area that lay immediately below the peak of the roof. It had no ceiling; only the underbelly of the roof itself, supported by a complex array of massive wooden beams. This was the highest point in the castle, and just before sunset on this fine winter's day, one small window offered a breathtaking view of the castle grounds, the forest and the district beyond.

They turned from the window and started to move across the dimly lit room. They found that it was almost empty, and were surprised by the few items that were there. Standing alone in the faint light near the centre of the floor was a small, antique card table surrounded by four wooden chairs. A solitary pile of old-fashioned playing cards sat neatly on the table, and the entire setting was covered by a thick layer of dust.

"This must have been here for ages," said David. "But why would they play cards all the way up here?"

Jason said nothing – his gaze fixed on the pile of cards. Suddenly, he picked them up, wiped the dust off the top one and placed it face-up on the table. Unexpectedly, they discovered it was not a playing card, but in fact a picture card. On it was an old illustration of the castle itself, covered in snow, just as it had appeared to them when they arrived. David was intrigued, but also started to feel uneasy. He recalled they were told not to touch anything, and his instinct said that this table setting in particular should not be disturbed.

Jason remained focused solely on the cards, and he placed another one down. It revealed a strange picture of two lambs standing before the castle door.

"I don't think we should do this," David said. "Let's just put them back."

Jason did not respond, and seemed entirely captivated by the cards in his hand. He continued to place three more upon the table. They showed a picture of a knight on a magnificent black horse; then a penitent man bowing before a noble lady; and finally, a beautiful, dark-haired woman holding an ornate metal cup at her breast.

These images were unlike anything they had seen before, and although David found them fascinating, he struggled to make sense of the cards. And now, even more so, he was concerned that they had been disturbed by Jason's meddling.

"Jason, we can't touch this. Put them back," he said again.

Jason slowly looked up from the cards and stared vacantly at his friend.

"Jason, I'm telling you, put them back now!" David shouted. He grabbed Jason's arm, took the cards from his hand, and began to return them all to their original position on the table. "What the hell are you thinking?" he said. "We were told not to touch anything."

127

"I'm sorry," said Jason, shaking his head. "That was very strange. I don't know why I did that."

"Okay, don't worry, let's get out of here. It's almost dark and I'm getting cold."

"Yeah, you're right – it's freezing up here."

With a shiver and briskness in their step, they left the attic and made their way down to the warmth and light on the second floor. There they met Eva, who took a small break from cleaning the hallway. They told her about all the things they had found in the attic, and asked if she knew anything about the old card table on the upper level.

"No, I never saw that room up the top," she said. "I have seen the window from the outside, but I certainly don't like to go all the way up there. The whole attic is too dark and dusty for me, and we don't rent space there. Just one time, Hans and I, we did look from the doorway, but we don't go further. It is interesting, all the old possessions of the Baroness, and it's good that you see it. Must be a lot different from what you have in your home, yes? I think some things are there for a very long time. Maybe some furniture and clothing from the early days of the castle."

Eva then excused herself, saying she must finish her work and would meet them later for drinks before dinner. She said they were welcome to chat with Hans who was preparing in the kitchen downstairs. They realised that the second floor was mainly occupied by their hosts, so they continued down to the first floor.

This was the location of the Baroness's apartment, and much of the floor was sealed off behind ornate, varnished doors. The large central hallway, however, remained accessible and they found it was being used as a gallery. There were dozens of old portraits on each side – all traditional oils with lavish wooden frames, often gilded. Many were so old that the years had embedded the artist's work with a sprinkling of fine cracks.

There was nothing humorous or casual in the gallery. All the portraits were formal records of the men, women, and sometimes children associated with the castle. Each one seemed to calmly challenge the viewer, gazing straight back at them, silently confirming they once lived here and were not to be forgotten.

David found them interesting but also a little chilling, as their collective gazes followed him slowly along the hall. Jason, however, seemed to find many of them rather amusing. He began to make fun of their facial features and serious expressions, and was often scornful of their constrictive and flamboyant clothing. One portrait in particular took Jason's attention – a large picture of an elderly, grey-haired woman, dressed quite regally and wearing a jewelled tiara.

"God, will you look at this old battle-axe!" he said, chuckling. "If she smiled, her face would split – pompous old prune. There are more cracks in that face than in a field of dried mud! Could you imagine being married to that?"

David had been trying to ignore his friend, but this last comment did stir a response. "Jason, will you please remember that most of these people probably lived here, and I presume they're ancestors of the Baroness, who's *still* living in the rooms right next to us."

"Yes, yes," said Jason, dismissively. "Come on, it's no big deal – just a bit of fun. Let's go and see Hans. I think it's time we checked the cellar." As he turned and headed down the stairs, his laughter could still be heard throughout the gallery.

Before David followed, he took another quick look at the hallway. So many portraits over so many years, he thought. For ages they'd all been hanging there, calmly and quietly staring at each other. For some vague reason, he now felt a kind of warmth and comfort in the old portraits. There was something there – something elusive he couldn't quite grasp.

They sampled the delights of the cellar, sharing a smooth pils and a strong dark beer with their hosts before dinner. In the coming months, the large dining room on the ground floor would be filled with patrons. However, on this night there was only the four of them sitting comfortably around a small table by the fireplace. Hans had prepared a most superb dinner of venison and roasted vegetables, covered in a rich sauce made with berries from the forest. This was accompanied by red wine, and followed by a wonderful selection of cheeses and hand-made chocolates. In the glow and warmth of the fire, the small party shared joyful conversation well into the evening.

Around eleven o'clock the young men said goodnight to their hosts and headed to their room. They were both feeling very full, merry and thoroughly satisfied with the day. The old bed had been prepared with fresh sheets, and Jason's portable was set up near the centre of the room.

David climbed up onto his bed, tucked himself beneath the thick quilt and let his head sink into the pillow. Feeling tired and very cosy, he quickly descended into a deep and mysterious sleep, unlike any sleep he had ever known.

Jason took a few more moments to get comfortable in his bed, then also drifted off.

Outside, the night remained clear and perfectly still. The silent grounds lay frozen beneath their cloak of snow, and only a few small lights from the castle pierced the darkness of the surrounding forest.

Shortly after midnight, Jason awoke feeling very cold. He immediately discovered he was unable to move – his body seemed fixed to the bed and he couldn't turn or get up. He was shrouded in absolute darkness, with not even a hint of starlight entering through the window. Although he was aware of the bed beneath him, he felt no coverings and thought his quilt must have fallen away.

Then he heard a slight creaking from the door, and for several seconds an icy breeze blew over him from head to toe. He wanted to call out but was struggling to breathe and couldn't murmur a word. He tried to turn his head towards the door, but still couldn't move. Every rigid fibre in him wanted to break free, and his heart pounded as a mysterious force from within the darkness bore down upon his chest, pressing him into the bed. He lay frozen with fear, feeling completely exposed and staring into a pitch-black void.

130

By the doorway he could hear the sound of women whispering, but was unable to discern anything being said. There was a brief moment of faint laughter, some further whispering, and then complete silence. He waited in dread, not knowing what to expect – the silence unbearable.

Finally, it was broken by the sound of someone walking towards him through the darkness. The steps came very close, and then moved slowly past his bed. He felt the gentle brush of fabric, like that of a dress or a robe, pass across his face and sweep along the length of his body. The steps moved away in the direction of the big bed, and although he felt a moment of relief, for the first time he wondered what was happening to David.

Then, from the doorway, he heard the stern and crackling voice of an elderly woman. It was sharp and clear, but seemed to be some kind of dialect, and he understood nothing. The voice rose steadily through the enclosing darkness, gradually coming nearer and nearer, till it became obvious that she was speaking to him alone. He remained terrified, sensing she must now be standing directly above him. After a moment's silence, he caught a whiff of old, musky perfume and suddenly felt her cold breath upon his cheek. He realised that her face must now be within inches of his. Then, with a heavy accent, the woman whispered a few short words of English in his ear.

"*You are my guest, young man . . . so be polite.*"

He felt the press of firm, cold lips upon his forehead. He fainted.

Part 2 – The Residents

Throughout Jason's ordeal, David continued to sleep tranquilly in the old bed. As the cool air spread slowly across the room, he remained warm and snug, and was peacefully unaware of all that was happening in the darkness around him.

The young woman had come to him and waited patiently until her mother left the room. She felt a degree of misgiving, and being so close to her bed again after all these years, made her feel a little melancholy. The bed had been a wedding gift from her husband, whom she loved so dearly. He came from a noble family living in the same district, and his father and hers had been strong friends and allies for many years. The closeness of their families meant that since early childhood their parents had warmly approved of their friendship. From the age of seven, he had been sent to live at their residence in order to provide personal service to her family. For many years, they were often playing games, engaged in sport or being tutored together, and at times they became quite inseparable.

However, at the age of fourteen he became a squire. He was sent away for further training in the military arts, and during a separation of almost seven years she missed him terribly. Upon his return as a young man, he had already received his knighthood for acts of bravery during a short campaign in the east. Together again, they soon discovered that their great friendship had become something much more.

She found him not only handsome, but loved his generous spirit and the respect he granted her. She admired him, too, for his courage and passion. He celebrated her immense beauty, and her love of

132

nature and the outdoors. Above all, he valued her good humour, free thinking and calmness of mind. They both knew, in the eyes of God, they had a love that would never be broken.

Their parents believed that a marriage between the two families would be of great benefit to all, and his proposal was given instant approval. Having gained such consent, she considered her life most blessed, for she recognised that very few were fortunate enough to marry in love.

Their three months of engagement were some of the happiest times she had ever known. They would go hunting or ride together when the weather permitted. Often, she would watch him in training with his colleagues, and she would always attend his tournaments. When indoors, they shared a love of music, poetry, and of reading the books their families had acquired.

Upon the celebration of their marriage, they took residence in the castle, which was bestowed to them as their new home by her uncle, the Duke. They shared the bed on many occasions, and she anticipated a time when she could announce she was with child. With this, she believed her life would be near perfect.

Regrettably, the time they had together after their marriage was short. Within six months, the word came that a company of knights was being quickly assembled to contribute to a large campaign on foreign soil in the north-east. Her husband was bound by his sacred duty and by his allegiance to her uncle. Within days, he joined others from the region and went off to fight the enemies of the faith.

Only a few weeks after his departure, she confirmed that she was carrying their child. Although she knew her husband would not be present at the birth, she greatly looked forward to when she could present him with their newborn upon his return. However, towards the end of her term she realised that her baby had ceased to move, and soon after this, she gave birth to a beautiful boy who failed to wake and breathe. The immense sorrow of her stillborn child was a burden most painful, yet she resolved that the will of God should not be challenged, and she remained confident of further opportunities.

133

At this time, she missed her husband more than ever, and longed for him each day as she awaited his return. But after an absence of a year, he had not returned as planned, and in solitude she wandered the corridors and grounds of the castle, fearing the worse. When, after several more months, she finally received confirmation of his death, she was devastated by grief, and resolved to never sleep in the bed again.

For a while she continued to live somewhat reclusively within the castle, and received great support from her mother, who spent more time there than in her own residence. Yet, her heart had been broken by the enormity of the loss, and although still young, she had no desire to remarry. Upon her death a year later, she believed she would be reunited with her husband. However, he never came to her, and she was unable to find him.

For almost six hundred years she had drifted among her family's castles in the region, but usually preferred to stay at her old home in the hope that one day he would return.

In the early days she was often visited by her grandmother and great aunt, and when her mother also passed away, the four of them would regularly meet to make use of the cards in the attic. Her grandmother had recommended them, having great confidence in their ability to assist in the search for her husband. However, for several decades the cards failed to provide any assistance, so they were eventually abandoned. Finally, she had to accept that his soul had been lost forever in a distant land.

Now she stood by her bed again and focused carefully on the young man who lay there so peacefully. Her mind was full of mixed thoughts and feelings.

During the previous afternoon, she had been walking by the lake when her mother suddenly appeared. They both sensed that something unusual was happening, and looked on with excitement as the horseless carriage entered the castle grounds and passed directly by them.

Together, they had followed the men to the front door and listened carefully as they introduced themselves to the new tenants. As she looked upon the one called David, her heart began to race. Her mother took her by the hand and swore that it was him – that her husband had finally returned. She moved in very close and studied his face. It was true. His hazel eyes and warm smile were the same she had loved, and he bore a striking resemblance in every other detail. However, his clothes were so ragged, his hair so short, and his German so poorly spoken.

They had decided to accompany the men throughout their tour of the castle. In the bedroom she was reassured by his strong fascination with the bed, and somewhat relieved that his friend did not wish to sleep there also. He then seemed to move about the castle with enthusiasm and confidence, and she was impressed by how quickly he had taken the stairs to the attic. Her mother, who had struggled to keep up, commented supportively that he has an adventurous spirit and clearly feels at home.

They stayed close to the men as they moved through the attic. They had hoped David would find her wedding dress, which had been resting for centuries in an old chest, but he passed right by it without lifting the lid. She wished the young men were not so compliant with the instructions given to them by Hans. Why should they not touch and play with anything that was there? She knew the Baroness wouldn't mind. She longed to take David's hand and lead him back to her wedding dress, but feared such contact would only shock him and he may leave. So, they followed on patiently without disturbing them.

They had not expected the men to find the cards so easily. After all, no one had been up there for such a long time, and in recent years they were almost forgotten. Her mother, true to character, had become a little impatient and insisted on seeing some of them. She had given Jason some gentle direction, and finally the cards had been very revealing. They had displayed pictures of all of them – the two men, her mother and her. However, with the light being so low, and with David's reluctance to look further, both men had failed to see what the cards were really showing them. For the women though, their meaning was clear. He had returned.

They had remained by the card table as the men hurried from the attic, and had thought carefully as to whether they should turn more of the cards. Her mother was keen to do so, but she was not so sure. She remained apprehensive of the future. The images may be pleasing or they may create more pain. The women had much to do, but at that moment she wished to follow him further, so she drew her mother away.

They had re-joined the men as they made their way into the portrait gallery. She had stayed close to David's side and noted his interest in a number of the paintings. She was eagerly waiting for him to notice her own portrait, but just as they were approaching it, they were distracted by a chorus of ridicule and laughter further down the hallway. Her mother, who was standing by Jason at the time, was seen to grimace and bristle with indignation as he displayed his ill-mannered amusement with her portrait. She knew her mother well, and had ushered her immediately from the gallery before she could express her anger further. They had a brisk walk through the gardens as she urged her mother to show restraint. However, the insult was deep, and it took a further three circuits of the lake to calm her completely.

Throughout the evening, as the men had dinner with the tenants, she and her mother sat in the Baroness's chambers and continued to discuss the matter. Finally, after much deliberation, they had reached decisions which were not quite satisfactory to either of them. They agreed that she alone must decide upon the best way to make contact with David, and her mother was free to deal with Jason, on the condition that he would come to no harm.

Now, at last, she stood alone beside him. She had thought about this moment for such a long time, and now it had come, she wasn't sure what to do. She yearned to be close to him again – to talk, dance, ride horses, make love – but now they stood on different ground. If he had come back to her in the spirit world, as she had hoped, she would have been fully prepared. However, he had returned in the flesh, from another time and another place, and his ignorance of his previous life presented her with some unforeseen difficulties.

Her mother had employed some of the more traditional methods of revealing herself and expressing her displeasure with Jason. However, with David, there was no such desire to cause alarm. She only wished that he would recognise his past, and appreciate that she had been waiting. But how was she to reintroduce herself and let him taste the life they had known?

If she were to wake him, no matter how compassionately, she feared it would only scare him. Encounters with the spirit world seemed less agreeable to people these days. And she did accept, regrettably, that her face was not as pretty as it once had been. The afterlife had taken its toll. Her skin remained smooth, but had turned to a pale grey. The rosiness had gone from her lips, and her cheeks were not as full. Her hair was no longer radiant, and her eyes retained only the slightest trace of blue.

So, she stayed there for quite some time, watching him so immersed in sleep. She stood there, thinking very carefully . . . and slowly she devised her plan.

He didn't feel the faint movement of the quilt over his chest, the gentle sway of the mattress, or the soft touch of her hand upon his face. Nor did he hear her delicate whispering at his ear, or feel her breath and the silky press of her lips upon his. However, with this touch he sank deeper into the void, to a place where the line between what is real and what is imagined is forever obscure. Then, guided by her, he became completely submerged in his reflected past and he began to dream – vivid and wonderful recollections of his adventures, knighthood, chivalry, their love and romance. Dreams which were so sensuous and fascinating that one would never wish to wake; and he didn't for many hours. He remained deep in sleep, caressed by the

137

images of his past, till the first rays of light entered the room the following morning.

He awoke slowly and lay quietly in the old bed for several minutes as the soft light gradually filled the room. He was surprised by how long and intensely he had slept, and felt completely invigorated and curiously fulfilled. He still felt so engaged with his dreams, that he wished he could sleep again and revisit them, but was too refreshed to do so.

He remembered that in the dreams he was a knight, living in the castle, and he had many adventures and was in love with a beautiful woman. But much of the fine detail was gone; lost in the haze of a slow transition to consciousness and waking to the morning light. It was very quiet, and as he sat up and threw back the quilt, he sensed a hint of perfume in the air.

He thought Jason must have already woken and left the room, but as he stepped from the bed, he noticed Jason was still lying there, fully awake, staring blankly at the ceiling.

"Oh . . . good morning," said David, cheerfully.

Jason continued to gaze at the ceiling and didn't say a word.

"Jason, are you okay? Did you sleep well?"

"When are we leaving?" Jason asked, almost whispering.

"Oh . . . maybe late morning. Get down to Munich in the afternoon. What's wrong?"

"Can't we leave straight away?"

"No! We're going to have breakfast, then I want to have another look around the castle, and I'd like to go for a walk in the grounds too. Jason, what's wrong?"

"I couldn't sleep very well, because . . ." He hesitated.

"Because *what?!*"

"Because . . . I was visited by a *ghost*."

"What? A ghost! Are you serious?"

"Yes . . . I'm dead serious. Actually, I think there were two of them – two women. I could hear them whispering to each other. One

138

of them went past me and went over to your bed. But then an old lady came to me . . . and she scared the shit out of me!"

"An old lady? How do you know it was an old lady? Did you see her?"

"No, it was completely dark – I couldn't see a thing. But I'm telling you, she spoke to me, and I could hear it was an old lady."

"What did she say to you?"

"She said a lot of things in German and I couldn't understand any of it. But then she spoke in English and said . . . I was her *guest*, and I have to be polite."

"Really? Why didn't you call out and wake me up?"

"I tried, but I couldn't say a thing! I couldn't move either – she had me fixed to the bed. And then, God-damn-it, she *kissed me!* She kissed me right here on the forehead with really cold lips. Urhhh!" He shivered uncontrollably for a moment. "I don't remember much after that – I must have passed out. When I woke up again, I couldn't get back to sleep and I was too afraid to move, so I just lay here. The whole thing was spooky as hell."

David frowned a little. "Hold on, let's get serious. If she said you're her *guest*, this is not a ghost. This must be the Baroness. We haven't seen her, but we know she's around. She's probably really old and we don't know what sort of crazy things she gets up to."

"No, there's no way this was the Baroness. I can't believe that. This was something completely different. I'm telling you – this was not a real person! Something powerful had me pinned to the bed and I couldn't do a thing. Her voice sounded terrible and her lips were like ice. You need to listen to me – it was a ghost from this castle – and I've never been so bloody scared." He lowered his voice. "I think it was the old lady in the portrait upstairs. It must have been her. She paid me back for what I said. God, I was stupid."

"Well, I don't really believe in ghosts, but if there are ghosts here, it doesn't surprise me. You were pretty rude to that one. And I did warn you in a way, didn't I?"

139

"Yes . . . you did," Jason whispered. "But didn't anything happen to you? You must have realised something was going on."

"No, I didn't meet any ghosts, if that's what you're asking. But I did have the most amazing dreams – really strong, colourful ones – almost like I was there, actually living them. So, I can see you're a bit spooked by all this, but I don't think what you felt was real. I think you were dreaming, just like me. This castle's affecting us a bit, and we did have quite a lot to drink last night. The only difference is that I had some really nice dreams, and yours were obviously really scary."

Jason shook his head and sighed. "I'm telling you – I wasn't dreaming. I was fully awake and this was real. I could hear them; I could feel them . . . I could even smell them!"

"Okay," said David. "C'mon, let's go to breakfast. We'll see what Hans and Eva have to say about it."

At breakfast they told their hosts what had happened to each of them during the night. Hans and Eva both laughed, saying it was not the first time the combination of an old castle and Bavarian beer had affected innocent tourists in such a way. With regard to Jason, they said they had heard rumours of ghosts within the castle but took little notice, since such rumours and speculation seemed to be associated with virtually every castle in the region.

Before they left for Munich, the young men decided to revisit the first floor. With a degree of hesitation, Jason moved slowly from portrait to portrait, apologising sincerely for his lack of courtesy and begging forgiveness. He remained nervous as he faced up to each, but became particularly apprehensive as he approached the portrait of the elderly, grey-haired woman. He realised that it was to her, above all, he must apologise. He found it difficult to look her in the eyes, so he bowed his head and spoke softly. He knew, without a doubt, she was listening carefully to every word.

As David waited for his friend, he wandered further down the hallway, glancing at the portraits once more. Near the door to the

Baroness's apartment, he noticed a very old portrait which he had not seen the previous day. It was of a young and beautiful, dark-haired woman, dressed elegantly in a crimson robe. He felt an intense and inexplicable attraction to her, and stood silently gazing for several minutes. He had a vague impression of having seen her somewhere before, but as much as he tried, he couldn't place it. As he stood before her, she sat peacefully within the old gilded frame, her gentle eyes looking back at him, with just the slightest hint of a smile upon her face.

When Jason finished his task, he was keen to leave. David, however, was reluctant to move away, and told his friend he wanted more time. Jason said he would collect their luggage and meet him outside at the car when he was ready. He then left the gallery and went downstairs.

David stood alone in the hallway and studied the portrait again closely. The artist had taken such care with every touch of the brush. The texture of her skin was like fine porcelain. Her neck, the line of her jaw, and her cheeks, were all soft and elegant. Her lips were rosy and full. Her glistening, dark hair was set formally, high upon her head, and her eyes were the blue of sapphire.

"She's beautiful, isn't she?" said a calm voice from behind him.

David turned around to see a woman standing a few metres away in the hallway. He was surprised that he had not heard her approach. She was in her seventies, conservatively dressed, with fair skin and light-grey hair tied in a bun at the back. She stood there, just smiling at him in the most welcoming fashion. He took a moment to gather his thoughts, and realised it could be no one else.

Part 3 – The Baroness

"Are you the Baroness?"

"Yes," she said with a courteous nod. Then she looked back towards the portrait. "So, do you agree?"

"Oh . . . yes! She's *very* beautiful. Probably the most beautiful woman I've ever seen."

"Her name was Katarina Maria Louisa Augsburg, and she was one of the first people to live in this castle. That was in the early fourteen-hundreds . . . and that's her mother over there." She pointed to the picture that had been of such concern to Jason.

David felt intrigued. Although she had a strong accent, her English was excellent, and she had given him, not only a name but also a date for the young woman's face.

"That long ago," he said. "That's incredible. The portrait is in such good condition."

"Yes, it's very special. I take good care of it . . . and, please, you may call me Charlotte."

"Oh, I should introduce myself. My name's David. I've been travelling with a friend – he's downstairs now. We stayed here last night."

"Yes, I know. I like to know everything that happens in the castle. And I understand you're from Australia."

"Yes, from Sydney."

"Hmm, interesting city. Is your family living there also?"

"My dad still lives in Sydney, but other than that, I don't really have much family. My mum died when I was born, and I don't have any brothers or sisters."

"Oh, I'm very sorry to hear about your mother."

"That's okay. It was hard for dad, but of course I never knew her. I do have some old photos, but that's about all."

Charlotte paused, and looked off down the hallway for a few seconds, glancing at the rows of faces on each side. "Tell me David; have you enjoyed your time here in the castle?"

"Yes, it's been great. We don't have places like this back home. I love it here."

"So, did you manage to take a tour?"

"Well, yes . . . we did have a small look around yesterday. Hans said it was okay, so I hope you don't mind. We looked inside your attic. Just amazing, all the things you have up there. We didn't touch anything of course."

She was still smiling and nodding gently, and he was delighted that he seemed to have her approval, and was actually showing some interest in him. She seemed so friendly, and he was feeling very much at ease in her presence. He thought for a second whether he should ask her about the cards, but decided it was probably a subject best avoided.

"And then," he continued, "we came down here and had a look at these portraits. Then, last night, Hans made us a superb dinner and we slept in the guest room. I slept in that huge, old bed."

"Ah yes – the bed. Did you sleep well?"

"Yes, I did, thank you. But my friend Jason, not so well. He got a bit spooked – thinks he met some ghosts. I just think he drank too much."

"Yes . . . perhaps he did. But you say you slept well."

"Yes, I had a brilliant night – slept so deeply and didn't wake up till morning. And I had the most incredible dreams. I've never dreamt like that before."

"Really? Dreams?"

143

"Yes. It's obviously something to do with staying here. It was like a long series of dreams, and I was a knight, living here in the castle. Can you believe it? I had armour and a huge horse – all that sort of stuff. I had lots of adventures." He paused, smiling, and gave a small chuckle. "And I remember I was in love too."

"In love? Oh, that sounds interesting – tell me more."

He stared at the floor, took a deep breath and closed his eyes, thinking hard. "I can't quite remember, but I know I was in love. There was a woman – a beautiful, extraordinary woman. We shared so many things together . . . and she . . . she . . ."

His eyes opened wide, and he turned and looked back at the portrait of Katarina. "Oh, my God!" he exclaimed. "I know this sounds strange, but I think it was her. This woman in the portrait – she was the woman in my dreams. Yes, I can see her clearly. I'm sure it was her. But I hadn't seen this portrait till just now."

Charlotte smiled again. "And, tell me, what did she do in your dreams?"

"Well . . . it's only just coming back to me . . . let me think. At one stage, I remember we were riding horses together, through the countryside, and we rode deep into a forest. And later, I remember there was a large banquet with lots of people, and we were sitting at the head of the table. She seemed so beautiful to me, and she was dressed in the most magnificent gown. Yes, I remember now. We danced – a very traditional dance – just me and her. Then we drank some wine, which we shared from a silver cup. I know it's hard to believe, but it was definitely her."

"David, it's not hard to believe," said Charlotte. "In fact, I would thoroughly expect Katarina to be the one who was with you in your dreams. Because, after all, you were sleeping in her bed."

"No! . . . Really?!"

"Yes, absolutely – the oldest and most special bed in the castle. It belonged to her and her husband . . . and he was a knight too."

He stood there, somewhat bewildered, and shook his head. "But how can I dream about Katarina if I never saw her before? And if it

144

was her, then I must have been dreaming about her and her husband, the knight. But it looked like me. It's all very strange, isn't it?"

"Maybe not as strange as you think. Katarina was a kind and intelligent woman, but unfortunately, she died quite young – soon after this portrait was painted, I believe. Apparently, she took her own life after the death of her husband on a foreign battlefield, far away from here. She loved him dearly . . . so you could say she died of a broken heart. And because her husband never returned to her, we believe, after all these years, that she's still here in the castle, waiting for him. So, you never know; since you saw both Katarina and yourself last night as you slept in her bed, maybe she thinks you are her husband. Maybe, she wants to show you something."

David pondered upon what the Baroness had just said. This was something he had not encountered before. That in the depth of his sleep, in such an old castle, he may have had contact with someone from the past.

"Do you really believe she's actually here in the castle . . . like, as a ghost?" he asked.

Charlotte gave a small laugh. "Well, it would appear so. How else do you explain that you saw her last night? David, I believe there are spirits all around us. It's an aspect of our lives that we don't fully recognise, but it's true. There are links between our lives and the lives of those in the past that we are only just beginning to comprehend."

"So, have you ever seen Katarina or any other ghosts in the castle?"

Charlotte still seemed a little amused, and glanced at the portrait once more. "Have I ever seen them? you ask. Let's just say that over the years I've become very well acquainted with them, and their special relationship to the castle. It's just a normal part of living in a place like this. Often, you feel the presence of others around you, and yes, occasionally, I have seen them. But, please understand, there's no need for you to be frightened. I've lived here all my life, and I've never had a problem with any of the ghosts."

He gazed vaguely through the gallery. "Real ghosts . . . here," he said to himself, and then turned back to the Baroness. "That would certainly explain what happened to Jason. But he believes he had quite a *problem* with them last night."

"Well, maybe he gave them cause to get a little upset."

"Yes . . . I guess he did. But you're right about Katarina. She's not at all frightening. She's just like in the portrait. I have to say – this castle is something I never expected. It's just unbelievable."

"Yes, it is truly a fascinating place to live. There are many surprising aspects to the castle that are not always obvious to the casual observer. In addition to Katarina in your dreams, you may have already seen some other strange things." She paused and looked at him intently.

"That's true," he admitted. "We did find some very interesting cards up in the attic – up the very top, just under the roof."

"Yes, I had a feeling you may have found those old cards. Intriguing, aren't they? They've been sitting up there for ages, covered in dust. They're a wonderful remnant of the past. This castle is simply full of remnants."

"What were the cards used for? They've only got pictures on them."

"Yes, they're quite puzzling. Some kind of medieval game, I suspect."

"But, do you know who put them there?"

"No – they've just always been there. A mysterious but rather charming feature of the castle, don't you think? And they don't get in the way, so we leave them there."

David took a moment to consider his time in the castle. "The attic and the cards, my dreams in the old bed, this portrait and the ghost of Katarina – I'm so glad I came here," he said.

"Yes, so am I. You and your friend are the first real visitors we've had for a very long time. I'm pleased you enjoyed your stay."

"Yes, I won't forget it. Thank you so much for having us."

"It has been my pleasure," Charlotte said, and for a moment, she gazed down the hallway, deep in thought. Then she gave him a somewhat inquisitive look and said, "But you know, there's a lot more to discover in the castle. There are many more interesting things I could show you, and I'd be very happy if you could return. If you wish to do so, you would come back as my special guest. Do you think you would like to do that?"

He was surprised, but also intensely excited by this unexpected and generous offer. "Yes!" he said. "I'd love to come back . . . but I'm not so sure about Jason."

"Oh, I don't think Jason wishes to spend more time in the castle. Why don't you finish your travels with him, then come and visit us again. Do you plan to go somewhere after Munich?"

"Yes, we're heading back to Paris. My trip with Jason finishes there in about two weeks, when we return the car."

"And after Paris?"

"Jason's going to visit some relatives in London, and I was planning to stay in Paris for a while, but that's not important. I've seen enough of Paris."

"Excellent. When you've finished with Jason, I'd like you to call me and I'll arrange a flight for you to Munich. Then I'll have you picked up from the airport."

"You would *fly* me back to Munich?"

"Yes, of course. I did say you would be my special guest."

"Oh, that's extremely kind of you."

"Good, that's settled then. Here's my card. Do call me from Paris. I look forward to your return very much." She handed David a small, white business card on which was printed the name 'Baroness Charlotte Von Ritterfeld' and the details of the castle.

"Thank you," he said, placing the card in his pocket. "This is so generous, but I must ask – why me? Why invite me as a special guest?"

She studied him carefully. "Well, it's obvious to me that you have a strong and unique connection with Katarina – a link that

147

perhaps we don't fully appreciate yet. When you return, that's something we could explore."

He thought again of how Katarina had appeared to him in his dreams, and of how exhilarating they were. "Yes . . . I'd like that very much," he said.

Then, for a few seconds Charlotte glanced admiringly between David and the portrait. "David, I believe it was your destiny to come here. You were destined to see Katarina in your dreams, and to finally recognise her portrait. Just like it's your destiny to find yourself in this gallery and to talk to me."

He was trying to gather what she was saying. He wasn't too sure about this idea, and was thinking it was probably just good fortune that he and Jason had seen the sign on the old highway. But he did like the idea of some kind of connection with Katarina. He loved the castle deeply and would not miss an opportunity to return.

"To think about one's destiny certainly is a strange thing," he said slowly. "I'm not sure if I really understand it – the forces that lead us on a certain path. All I know is that it's been wonderful to be here, and I feel really excited about coming back."

"Well, your return will be greatly anticipated," Charlotte said.

He thought for a moment. "And when I return, would I be sleeping in the guest room?"

"Yes, of course. That room is definitely reserved for you. I'll make the arrangements with Hans and Eva . . . and I think we should keep our knowledge of Katarina and her mother to ourselves. That can be our secret – we won't tell the others. It would only complicate things if they were to know."

"Yes, I won't mention it."

"Very good. Now you'll have to excuse me. There are many things I have to prepare, and soon you must depart for Munich with Jason." She paused briefly. "I also think it's best you don't tell Jason we've spoken. He may not understand."

"Yes, I agree."

"Now, I believe Hans and Eva will be waiting downstairs, and I know they have something for you." She held out her hand to him. "Till we meet again."

"Thankyou Charlotte," he said, and he took her hand. As he did so, she looked over his shoulder to the portrait of Katarina and gave another of her gracious smiles. He turned around and looked at the portrait once more.

"I think . . ." He started to say something as he turned back to the Baroness, but then discovered she was gone. He thought he heard a faint 'click' from the door to her apartment. Scanning the length of the hallway, he saw nothing but the light from a far window and the dozens of faces hanging silently on each side.

"Auf wiedersehen," he whispered.

Then he stood there in the midst of the gallery and thought about all that had transpired with the Baroness. So much had happened in that short time, and he was still trying to come to terms with everything she had said.

A few metres away, by the door to the Baroness's apartment, Katarina and her mother stood arm in arm. They had been there for some time, calmly observing the proceedings.

Earlier, her mother had followed Jason as he made his way down the hall. When he came to her portrait, she had witnessed his apology with a great deal of satisfaction. She had been tempted to give him another kiss, or perhaps a small whisper in his ear, but then thought the poor boy had suffered enough. Besides, if her actions had interrupted David at that time, her daughter would never have forgiven her.

They had watched David as he found Katarina's portrait, and had listened carefully to his conversation with Charlotte. She had been such a good friend, managing the situation perfectly, and they were now delighted with how the day had progressed.

They continued to stand there, as there was still one moment they had been patiently waiting for.

149

It was now late morning, and the winter sun crept steadily along a low arc to the south. It was hidden behind a broad band of clouds, but had risen sufficiently above the height of the surrounding forest, so that when the clouds parted, it brightly illuminated the front of the castle. It shone directly through the far window of the hallway, bouncing sunlight off the heavily varnished flooring, which then scattered its way through the entire gallery.

What had been dimly lit by a series of small tungsten lamps, now sprang to life with full colour in the brilliant sunshine. Skin tones of ivory and pink; furs of cream and beige; glistening rubies and emeralds; satins and velvets in burgundy, purple, deep forest green and royal blue. Every person, every garment, and every piece of regalia, now seemed to leap from the ancient frames and warmly greet the young man that stood amongst them.

David was struck by the beauty of this perfectly illuminated scene. He took a deep breath and turned about slowly to take it all in. It appeared that every face was focused on him. His gaze followed the sunlight from the window, down past the portrait of Katarina, to the very end of the hallway. There stood a large crystal vase upon an old hallstand. Shards of light dispersed upwards through the vase and splashed across the front of one last portrait that hung there. Modest in size, with a thick gilded frame that shone brightly back at him, it was only about ten metres from where he was standing. However, he had been so preoccupied with Katarina's portrait and his conversation with the Baroness, he hadn't noticed it till now.

He was drawn to the portrait, and then stood gaping and motionless before it. The armour was a radiant silver and meticulously crafted. A gold chain and cross hung over the breastplate. An ornate and sturdy helmet sat on a small side table, on which was draped a cloth with coat-of-arms. While one hand rested on the helmet, the other lay on the hilt of a large sword, slung from the waist. Long, fine hair flowed down over the shoulders, and with

150

fair skin and confident eyes, the young knight's face was unmistakably his own.

Katarina felt her mother's arm tighten and draw her closer. They observed David as he stood there for several minutes, locked deep in thought. At times he would study the portrait in detail, then pause and stare pensively at the floor. Often, he would turn back to glance at Katarina's portrait, then return again to focus upon his own.

Slowly, the pieces were being assembled in his mind as he reviewed his moments in the castle. The attic and cards, the bed and his dreams, the gallery and the words of the Baroness. It all began to come together, and the complete realisation filled him with delight. This vital part of his identity – that which had been buried and lost – was now rediscovered. Gradually, his sense of pleasure turned to euphoria, and he released himself entirely to fate.

He turned and went back to Katarina's portrait, then slowly knelt before it. For a few moments he closed his eyes and bowed his head in reverence, knowing she must surely be near. Then he got up, looked about briefly and strode downstairs.

Katarina embraced her mother and kissed her on the cheek. Her mother gave her a smile that she had not seen since she was a young girl. They would make all the necessary arrangements with the Baroness, Katarina thought. And two weeks was not a long time to wait. Hardly any time at all, considering.

David went outside to the forecourt and driveway, where Jason and their hosts were talking as they waited by the car.

"Hey, Dave," Jason called as he approached. "Hans agrees – there really could be some ghosts here. There's been a couple of times when his chocolates have disappeared from the kitchen, and Eva swears it wasn't her."

David laughed, immediately suspecting the stealthy movements of the Baroness. "Well, I couldn't blame a ghost for wanting to try them," he said. "Hans, didn't you say people will be dying to eat your chocolates?"

They continued to chat for a couple of minutes, and the young men warmly thanked Hans and Eva for their great hospitality. Then Hans told them he had met the Baroness earlier that morning, and she had sent her very best wishes and hoped they found their stay interesting. He said she wanted them both to have a memento of their stay in the castle, and presented each of them with a small present, neatly wrapped and held by a ribbon.

Jason unwrapped his present first, and found a small and excellently-crafted wooden box. He opened the lid, and inside was a brand-new deck of playing cards. Each card was handsomely embossed in gold with the Bavarian coat-of-arms. He was a little surprised but quite pleased, and asked Hans to offer his thanks to the Baroness.

David pulled the ribbon on his present, and as the paper fell away, it revealed a beautiful, antique, silver cup. He studied it for a few seconds, and then quickly looked up to the first floor of the castle. In the main window above the front door, he thought he could recognise the hazy outline of three women standing side-by-side. Yet, he wasn't quite sure. The view through the window was partially obscured by a thin layer of ice and the reflections of distant clouds. He squinted and tried to focus. Still, it wasn't clear.

David guessed they must be watching, and he raised the cup in a gesture of respect. Then he turned back to Hans and told him to pass on his sincere gratitude.

The young men got into the car, waved goodbye, and drove off through the grounds.

Part 4 – The Return

The district was now immersed in the tranquil but intense cold of winter. There was not a breath of wind, and the forest lay still and quiet under a deeply overcast sky. Snow had been falling steadily throughout the morning and the fir trees were heavily laden, their branches hanging low and straining under the weight. The only sound was from the occasional bough that suddenly relinquished its load and sprang up as a mass of snow crashed to the forest floor. Then silence again.

In the early afternoon, a large, black BMW entered the castle grounds. David sat in the front passenger seat, calmly looking out across the frozen lake and to the castle beyond. Since leaving Munich, he had found it difficult to engage the somewhat elderly driver in any form of conversation. So, for the last hour, he had been content to be driven in silence while he surveyed a peaceful countryside cloaked in snow and ice.

Hans and Eva were waiting at the castle forecourt. As David got out of the car, Hans came forward to shake his hand. "Welcome David. It's wonderful that you return to stay with us. I didn't realise you became such a good friend of the Baroness. When she told us you would return, I was surprised, but very pleased to see you again."

"Yes, it's great to be back," David said. "This place is very special, and it's so kind of the Baroness to invite me . . . and also good to see you two again."

"How is your friend, Jason?" Eva asked. "Did he recover from his fear of ghosts?"

153

"Oh, yes, he's fine now. We talked about it a lot. He got quite a scare, but I assured him that since he apologised, all would be forgiven."

"Yes, of course," Eva said. "Did you tell him you were coming back?"

"No, I didn't want him worrying about that. He flew off to London yesterday and thinks I'm still in Paris."

The driver had taken David's bag from the boot and was waiting patiently to one side, not willing to put it down on the snow-laden driveway. Hans reached for it and the driver handed it over without saying a word. They shook hands briefly and Hans said "danke". Then the driver got into the car and drove off.

"A man of few words," David noted.

"Oh, don't worry about Klaus," Hans said. "He's a lovely old man, but he is – how do you say? – '*as deaf as a post*'. So, he doesn't like to speak much. Come on, let's go inside, out of the cold. We have the guest room ready for you, and you stay as long as you wish."

They entered the castle and were instantly cradled by its warmth. Looking down the central hallway, David could see the main fireplace near the base of the stairs was fully stoked and burning furiously. He felt his face begin to flush a little.

"Wow, you've got this place warm as toast," he said, taking off his coat.

"Yes, it holds the heat quite well," said Hans. "The Baroness wants you to be as comfortable as possible during your stay. Now, I think you must be quite hungry after all your travels today. Would you like me to prepare some lunch for you?"

"No, that's not necessary. I had some food on the plane."

"Well, I expect you'll be very hungry by tonight, which is good, because I'm preparing a *feast*. And of course, the Baroness will be joining us." Hans smiled with an air of pride.

"And, after you settle in," added Eva, "the Baroness would like to see you upstairs."

"Oh, yes, I look forward to that," said David.

"Good," said Eva. "Hans, help David by taking his bag to the guest room."

"Oh, please, I can take the bag myself. I remember where my room is. Thank you – both of you – thank you very much."

David closed the door and put his bag down in the corner. Then he sat at the end of the old bed and looked slowly about the room. Apart from the absence of the portable bed, it was exactly as it had been a fortnight earlier. The old bed was fully prepared and covered with the same thick quilt. The antique paintings and ornaments on the walls – all the same as before. Everything was in its place, and not a sound could be heard from outside or from within the castle itself. He felt a little apprehensive of the possibility that something may suddenly change. She must be here, he thought to himself. Surely, she would be eager to see him on his return. He let the thought linger and settle, as he waited for a moment. Still . . . an unchanging room, resting in complete silence.

"Katarina, are you here?" he whispered. He felt a little silly talking to a vacant room, but he sensed she must be there. "Katarina?" he whispered again, continuing to look around as he waited a little longer. There was nothing.

Enough, he thought – it's time to see the Baroness. As he rose from the bed and headed to the door, he caught the sweet scent of perfume drifting in the air. He paused and scanned the breadth of the room once more. "Katarina . . . I know you're here," he said with a small grin. "You're playing games, aren't you?" He waited a few more seconds, but still no response. He gave a small sigh and left the room.

As he made his way up to the first floor, he was expecting to knock on Charlotte's door and be invited in for a cup of tea or the like. He was really looking forward to seeing her apartment, being so sure it would be filled with antiques and other interesting items from the

155

past. However, as he came off the stairs and entered the gallery, he found her waiting for him patiently in the centre of the hallway.

"Charlotte!" he said. "You're here already. I'm sorry, I hope I didn't keep you waiting."

"Not at all. David, welcome home!" She moved forward and gave him a short embrace and kiss on the cheek.

"Yes . . . this was my home."

"Yes, it was. Come this way." With a somewhat playful look, she gestured for him to follow her down the hall.

The gallery was not as brilliantly illuminated as he had last seen it, but as he followed her, the temperate light of the hallway seemed to present the portraits with a warmth and charm he had not expected. For the first time, he began to fully realise the depth of the bond he had with each of them. At the far end, as they came to his own portrait, he started to feel the same wave of anticipation that he had two weeks earlier.

Charlotte placed her hand lightly upon his shoulder. "So, here you are, David – in a past life. This was your home, and this is where you still belong."

"Yes," he said, staring at the picture. "This *was* me. Deep down, I can feel it. Now I understand why I've always wanted to come to Bavaria – why it's been intriguing and tempting me for years. And I know why I saw myself with Katarina in the dreams, and why I feel so happy here." He stood deep in thought for a few seconds, and then looked back at Charlotte. "Have Hans and Eva seen this portrait?"

"No, I don't think so," she said, shaking her head. "They don't come to this end of the hallway. The stairs are too far away."

"They'd get a surprise if they did."

Charlotte smiled. "I expect so."

He focused on the portrait once more. "So . . . what was my name?"

"Would you like the whole name?" Charlotte asked. "You may find it a little unusual."

"Yes, tell me."

156

"Maximillian Theodore Eric Von Schramm."

"My God, that's a mouthful, isn't it," he said, amused.

"Yes, I agree. The name has some depth to it."

"And I was married to Katarina."

"You were friends since childhood, and were married for a short while."

"But then she took her own life after I was killed, and she's been waiting here all these years for me to return."

"Exactly. She thought at first, you would return in the spirit world, soon after your death, but that never happened. Then, she thought she would join you in death, but still she couldn't find you."

"And may I ask *how* she died?"

"Of course you may. She drowned herself in the lake – right here near the castle. It was very sad, and a great shock to the family."

"Oh, that is sad," he agreed. Then he thought for a moment. "But if she's been a ghost here in the castle all this time, why couldn't I come back to her as a ghost all those centuries ago?"

"That's a good question. We've asked ourselves that many times, and unfortunately, we can't be sure of the answer. Our only conclusion is that it may be something to do with the manner and location of your death. You see, David, in fourteen-hundred-and-ten, you went off to fight in a large campaign in Prussia – to an area which today is in northern Poland. The campaign culminated in a famous battle – the Battle of Grunwald. Have you heard of this battle?"

"No, not at all."

"It was unfortunately a rather tragic affair, especially for the Teutonic Knights. The battle was fierce and ruthless, and it became, as you would say, a 'bloodbath'. I have no doubt you fought bravely, but you, along with hundreds of knights and thousands of other soldiers were slaughtered. After it was done, your body was buried there, probably with little ceremony. So, we suspect that your failure to return had something to do with the horrible nature of your death and your burial so far from home."

157

He took a slow, deep breath and stared at his portrait. "Well, such is the fate of a knight," he said with calm resignation.

"Yes," Charlotte agreed. "But let's not dwell on these gruesome and depressing things. The fact is, here you are – returned at last. Although it's taken nearly six hundred years, Maximillian remains a strong part of you, and not just in the way you look. He is in every strand of your being, hiding just below the surface."

"Yes, I understand. And what about Katarina? I thought I could sense her presence downstairs in the bedroom, but she didn't reveal herself. Is it possible for me to meet her?"

Charlotte smiled at him. "Everything is possible, David. But I have found the actions of ghosts to be somewhat unpredictable. Let's go to the attic. I think we have our best chance up there."

As they headed to the stairs, Charlotte stopped briefly and gazed at the portrait of Katarina. "You know, David, I can't promise you'll see her. She can sometimes be a little playful and may keep you waiting. But I assure you, she's very keen to be with you."

As he looked at the portrait once more, he remembered the slight smile upon her face.

David followed Charlotte as she moved slowly through the attic. The air was cool but tolerable, as some of the heat had gradually filtered in from downstairs. He noted that since entering, she had been scanning the room from one side to the other, and occasionally glancing at the ceiling. She then began to stare at a row of large wooden chests that sat by some racks of old clothing near the centre of the floor. After a few moments, she looked back at him.

"So, is she here? Can you see her?" he asked.

"Yes, she is here," Charlotte replied, "and her mother and several others too."

He looked about rapidly. "Really! There are more? Where are they?"

"All about us, David. They surround us."

Scattered about the room were at least a dozen family members. Katarina's father had made a rare appearance, having come up from one of his favourite haunts in Munich specially for the occasion. Her uncle, a few cousins, grandmother and great aunt were also present. And, of course, Max's parents were there. They were naturally very excited by the prospect of seeing him again, and had interrupted their tour of the Black Forest in order to attend.

"My God. Should I say something to them?" David asked.

"If you wish, of course you may," said Charlotte. "They can hear you, but remember they all have little to no English."

"Oh . . . yes, I forgot about that." He gazed around the room and tried to think of something simple and appropriate. "Hello," he said finally. "Mein name ist David . . . well, in diese leben. Aber, Sie kennen mich as Maximillian." He felt awkward and turned back to the Baroness. "It would be easier if I could see them, or at least see Katarina."

Charlotte gave him a warm smile. "Don't worry, you don't need to say any more. They all understand the situation. Katarina remains hesitant to reveal herself entirely to you at this time. She prefers to see you as you sleep during the night. But there is something special she wishes to share with you now, and this is why the others have come."

"She wants to *share* something with me?"

"Yes. These wooden chests, here on the floor. I don't think you opened them when you were here two weeks ago."

He looked over at the chests. "No, we didn't. Hans told us not to touch anything."

"Hans means well, but he's far too polite. He made you too cautious. Katarina would love you to open that chest." She pointed at one of them. "That one there – the really old, dark one."

David moved forward and stood before the chest. "This one?"

"Yes, that's the one. Open it, please."

He bent down, unfastened the latch, and slowly lifted the lid. Inside, he could see the neckline and upper portion of a large, blue-coloured gown, neatly folded.

"Should I take this out?" he asked.

"No, David. It's better if you stand back a little."

He took a few steps back and stared intently at the open chest. He didn't know what to expect, and could feel his heart beating and his breath quicken.

Katarina left her mother's side and moved swiftly across the floor. For a brief moment, she looked back tenderly to where her parents and the others were standing. Then she turned and swung gracefully between the Baroness and her husband. She gave David a small kiss as she passed, and he was briefly startled by the light peck and gentle stroke of cool air upon his cheek. Holding back a joyful laugh, she then focused on the task ahead.

The gown began to stir, then slowly unfold and rise from the old wooden chest.

"Oh!" gasped David, taking a further step back. "Oh, my God."

On display to all gathered, the gown rose to shoulder height and remained suspended in the air for several seconds. It then began to swell and fill, and took advantage of every feminine proportion afforded by its design. Intricately woven in plush mid-blue velvet, with gold trim and an inlay of cream-coloured satin, it extended fully to the floor. Its tight bodice was round and firm in the bust, and narrowed in the waist. It was generous at the hips and widened to the hem. Its arms were long and draping, and at their finish were a pair of slender, silk gloves.

"As I told you," Charlotte said, "although you can't see her, Katarina is here."

David stood awestruck by the scene before him – his eyes fixed on the gown; his mouth partly open. "Yes . . . she is," he said slowly.

"Do you recognise the dress?"

"Yes . . . I've seen it before. It was in the dream. It's her wedding dress, isn't it?"

"Yes. Do you like it?"

"Of course. It's beautiful."

The gown's left arm raised slowly in the air, and the gloved hand turned to beckon David forward.

"I think Katarina would like to dance," said Charlotte.

"Oh, really?! But I haven't got a clue about traditional dancing. I'm a poor dancer at the best of times."

"Yes . . . she remembers. But still, she's been looking forward to this for some time."

The prospect of dancing with her like this, had him caught between feelings of pure elation and a fear of the unknown. He was certainly willing to try, but also quite sure he would fail to perform. "Perhaps Katarina could take the lead?" he suggested.

"A novel idea, David. I can only ask her." Charlotte leaned closer to the wedding gown and whispered, "Er möchte dass Sie führen." *("He would like you to lead.")*

The left arm stayed firmly in the air; then extended a fraction further.

"David, I think she considers that inappropriate. Too much of a departure from the norm – you understand?"

"Yes, I do. But seriously, I'm no good."

"Don't worry. Thankfully, *she's* excellent, and I'm sure you'll be right. Just follow your instinct."

Once again, the gloved hand turned upwards, beckoning him, and with a degree of apprehension, he stepped forward and gently held it.

At first, the sensation was bewildering. To have the gown stand alone before him; to see her shape form within it; then suddenly feel the delicate pressure of her hand against his, was something quite incomprehensible. He was speechless and had no idea what to do.

Katarina could instantly sense his unease. It was natural, she thought, that in an absence of six hundred years, one would get a little out of practice. And, if she were to be perfectly honest, she always knew his dancing had room for improvement. The talents he had in riding, swordplay and jousting, simply did not translate to the dance

161

floor. She recalled that their wedding dance required several days of painstaking preparation. So, with this in mind, she could not allow the possibility of her husband looking foolish in front of the family. This very special occasion would require something more – a greater form of artistic control.

From that first touch of her hand, as surreal as it was, he began to feel the true depth of her presence. She became at once tangible, and like the portrait, he found he could more easily visualise her standing beside him – her bright eyes, supple mouth and cheeks, radiant hair – no longer simply a dress, but now whole. Then, slowly, he felt an unexpected sensation of warmth generate from her glove and slowly infuse through him. It ran over his arms and chest, down through his torso and into his legs. Now entirely at her direction, she began to guide him effortlessly across the floor. To his surprise, he seemed to be acquainted with every step, and was quickly overcome by a delightful confidence as his arms and legs took on a life of their own. He found himself gliding and turning to one side, then the other. Forward steps, a rise and a fall. A backward step and a small bow. The Basse Danse repeated itself again and again – graceful, dignified, and by nature, truly Gothic.

Emanating from somewhere overhead, he could hear the gentle sound of medieval music. Was it some form of guitar and a flute? he asked himself. At this stage, however, he was so receptive to anything bizarre and ethereal, he couldn't be bothered to look for its source. Smiling broadly, he kept his eyes on his partner and warmly accepted the music as another fitting and extraordinary element that gave balance to the occasion.

Katarina could see her husband was now relaxed and greatly enjoying himself. She decided to introduce a few of the more flamboyant Italian variations – a light skip here, a small twirl there – even a brief parting of the hands. Her cousins had suggested these small extravagances, promising that her uncle would approve. She had known the Duke to be strictly conservative during his lifetime, but apparently in death, he had become quite a fan of the avant-garde.

With the changes, David soon heard small bursts of appreciation from around the dim edges of the room. The increasing chatter and moments of applause made him feel so pleased with how the dance was progressing, he couldn't help but laugh. Seeing him this way and sharing his pleasure, Katarina laughed too, and for the very first time, he heard her voice. The unexpected sound coming from the wedding gown surprised him, and he suddenly realised that till now, he hadn't thought to say anything.

"Are you happy?" he asked, as she next turned towards him.

She understood the question, but hesitated for a few seconds, thinking of how best to answer. He began to wonder whether she could comprehend. Then, as she made her next curtsy, she said, "So glücklich wie jetzt war ich schon seit Langem nicht." *("I haven't been this happy for a long time.")*

He also understood her, but more impressive to him still, was the sound of her voice. Its tone and accent immediately captivated him. It was deliciously feminine and alluring, and he felt a rush of desire that he had never expected.

"I am also very happy," he said.

She laughed again.

That was enough for Katarina's eldest cousin, Magdalena, a headstrong woman who'd been waiting patiently for an appropriate moment to join the dance. She took hold of her father's hand and led him across the floor. Seeing the Duke head out, spurred Max's parents into action, and they followed closely. Then, Katarina's father also gained some inspiration, and for the first time in ages, he managed to get his wife to the dance floor.

The dance continued for a few more minutes. As the music finished, David stood composed, holding Katarina's hand, and made his final bow. The vibrant sound of applause came from all around him, and much closer than he had expected. With the success of the dance and his love for Katarina, all he could feel was exhilaration. And Katarina, too, was thrilled. Having her husband at her fingertips at long last, she knew that all her hopes and plans had been justified.

As he stood there amid the applause, the gown moved to him and embraced him tightly. He placed his arms around her waist and pulled her in tight. He could feel her breasts, firm against his body; the press of her thighs against his; and the rhythmic movement of cool breath upon his neck. Again, he heard her voice, as she whispered in his ear. "Heute Nacht."

"Yes . . . *tonight*," he whispered in reply.

The sound of applause faded slowly into the dusky corners of the room, then finally disappeared. As it did so, the wedding gown collapsed in his arms, and he was left standing alone in the heart of the attic, cradling the now empty, lifeless dress. The only sound was from Charlotte, who walked over to him, joyfully clapping her hands.

"David, really . . . I thought you said you were a poor dancer. That was magnificent!"

He held up the dress, a mixed look of surprise and confusion on his face. "She's gone."

"Yes, that's right. She's gone now . . . and all the others. Remember I told you their actions are unpredictable. But don't worry, you'll see them again."

He carefully folded the dress and placed it back in the open chest. Turning to Charlotte, he said, "That was, without doubt, the most incredible thing I've ever done. But I'm sure you realise that Katarina took the lead after all."

"Well, I always knew she'd have the situation under control. But the most important thing is that you both enjoyed yourselves."

"Yes, she seemed very happy."

"More than happy – she had tears in her eyes."

"Oh . . . that's a beautiful thing," he said, then paused for a second. "And the rest of the family? I presume it was them clapping."

"Yes, of course. But, do you not realise? They were so delighted with your performance, they all joined in. It became quite a procession."

"Really! I had no idea."

164

Charlotte looked down at the open chest. She straightened out the top of the gown, then closed the lid and fastened the latch. "So, how do you feel about Katarina now?" she asked. "Do you think, like Max, that there may be a special place in your heart for her?"

"You mean, do I love her?"

Charlotte smiled. "Yes . . . that *is* what I mean."

He was a little surprised that she expected such candour, but then he thought it was only fair. "I never imagined a relationship as strange as this. I didn't think such things could be possible. But now, since you ask . . . I actually think I do love her."

"Oh, that's wonderful! You have my blessing." Charlotte stepped forward and gave him a small hug. "I'm so glad you've returned to the castle and found something so special." Then she thought for a second and glanced at the ceiling. "Now, I have an idea. Since we're in the attic, why don't we go up and have a look at those fascinating cards. I'd really like to see them again, and I'm sure they'll be of interest to you."

"Yes, that's a great idea. I was hoping you'd say that."

They started making their way to the smaller stairs at the far end of the floor.

"The cards are connected to the spirit world, aren't they?" he said. "They tell us things. But you already knew that, didn't you? I realise now, there were pictures of Maximillian and Katarina, but there's more – a lot more. I think they show us what is happening . . . and even what *will* happen."

"I believe you're right," Charlotte said. "I know they have a strong connection with the spirit world and all our friends in the castle. It will be interesting to see what they are showing us now."

The card table and chairs were standing exactly where he and Jason had seen them two weeks earlier. However, as they approached, he could clearly see there had been a couple of changes. Instead of a large pile of cards resting at the centre of the table, there was now only one. And the thick layer of dust that covered the entire setting had been cleaned away. It was all spotless – not a speck remained anywhere.

"They've been here," David said, a little puzzled. "They've taken all the cards, except for one. And it's like they've prepared it for us. Look – all the dust has gone." He stared at Charlotte for a moment, and then an inquisitive smile came over his face.

"Not me, David," she said. "I haven't been up here for years. Believe me, this is my least favourite part of the castle. From my experience, this is most likely the work of Katarina's mother. She very much likes to play a hand in things."

He gazed around the edges of the attic. "So, are you sure she's not here checking on us now? Come to think of it, are any of them here?"

"No, David. I can assure you, none of them are here. They're leaving us alone now. As I mentioned, and I think you confirmed, Katarina will see you tonight in your sleep."

"Yes, '*tonight*' she said."

"So now, I have just one question for you. Are you going to turn that card?"

He looked at the solitary card that lay face-down on the table. The back of it was tantalising him. Its intricate medieval pattern of red crosses and blue stars, embedded in a uniform grid of small white diamonds, was enticing him to reveal what lay beneath.

"For them to leave just this one, it must obviously be of great significance," he said. "So, of course, I must turn it." He reached out, raised one edge, and turned it over.

It was a picture of extraordinary detail – like that of a fine etching – with complex tones of light and dark, and all the delicate shades between. Through its centre ran a narrow stream of water, swift and turbulent, that cut a neat channel through a fertile, grassy field. On one bank stood Katarina, dressed in a flowing gown, peacefully reaching out with her hand over the water. On the other bank was David, kneeling by the verge of the stream, wearing the long tunic of a knight, emblazoned with a holy cross. While one hand was reaching toward Katarina, the other rested on the hilt of his sword, which stood upright beside him, driven into the grass.

Both David and Charlotte studied the picture closely. "It's very interesting," he said. "But I'm not really sure if I understand it. What do you think?"

"Well, I can't be sure either; but I can take a guess," Charlotte replied. "Clearly, we can see that you and Katarina are separated by the stream – perhaps the stream of time and misfortune. And we can also see that you're reaching for each other – that you both desire to have contact. But it's only a narrow stream, and it appears quite possible for you to touch each other. And we already know that – correct? Through the various forces in your life, you've managed to come all this way to the castle. And Katarina has found special ways to share her life with you, and even to hold you through the wedding dress."

"Yes, that sounds right. But why am I kneeling?"

"Hmm, good question. I think it's in the culture of a knight when he is honouring the woman he loves. Didn't you kneel before her when you were last here?"

"Yes . . . I did," he said, recollecting that moment in the gallery. "You saw that?"

Charlotte laughed and gave him a small wink. "David, I did mention once before, that it's my business to know everything that happens in the castle."

"Yes . . . of course. And what do you make of the sword? It being stuck in the ground."

Charlotte seemed a little puzzled and shook her head. "This, I really don't know. Knights are always sticking their swords in one place or another. Maybe it helps you balance by the edge of the stream, or maybe you've decided to leave it there. Perhaps it's put there to simply indicate that you once were a knight – I can't be sure. I don't think we should read too much into it. After all, as magical as it is, it's just a romantic image."

"Yes, you're right. The most important thing, is the picture clearly shows the strength of my relationship with Katarina."

"Absolutely," Charlotte agreed. "And tonight, you're going to *experience* the strength of that relationship. It will be wonderful, David. I'm sure the dreams you'll have tonight will seem more vivid and real than you can possibly imagine. They will be something of extraordinary beauty. And in the morning, I look forward to showing you more of the castle. I expect you'd like to see my apartment, and there are many other areas you haven't discovered yet. There's so much more to see." She pulled up the collar of her jacket and gave a small shiver. "But now I'm starting to feel the cold, and we must prepare for dinner, so let's go downstairs."

As they made their way from the upper attic, they stopped briefly at the landing above the steps and looked out the window. It had stopped snowing and the visibility was much improved. The heavily laden grounds and snow-capped forest extended for several hundred metres. Beyond that, the only thing moving was a small blue car passing slowly on the old highway in the distance.

"The view is breathtaking up here, isn't it?" said Charlotte. "I simply must come up here more often – especially in the summer. Perhaps the next time I'm up here, there'll be more cards available for viewing."

They continued down the steps and moved through the main floor of the attic once more. As they passed the row of old wooden chests, David thought again about his experience with Katarina and her wedding gown.

"It's incredible to think that the wedding dress is almost as old as the castle itself," he said. "Do you know where Katarina and Max were married?"

"Yes, I do," said Charlotte. "They were married in an old Gothic church about four or five kilometres from here. It had just been consecrated, and the wedding was the first to take place there. But unfortunately, the original church was destroyed by fire around seventeen-hundred, and it was completely restored in the Baroque style. It's located in a field on the other side of the town. It's really very beautiful."

"Oh, I've seen this church. I saw it with Jason when we first drove here. It's the one with a very tall tower, and it sits in a big field, all by itself – right?"

"Yes, that's the one."

"That *is* a beautiful church. I took a photograph of it."

"I'm so glad you saw it. You obviously recognised it was something very special, and I'm sure you'll treasure the photo. There are no photographs of the original church, of course, but I do have a painting. It was also very beautiful."

Charlotte led the way from the attic and they went down to the first floor, where they stopped outside her apartment.

"I noticed the church had a graveyard," David said. "Katarina and the other early residents of the castle – is that where they're buried?"

"I was wondering when you'd ask that question," Charlotte said, glancing down the hallway for a second. "I don't know of any who are buried there. All the people you speak of – those in the portraits here – are buried in a very old graveyard, just a short distance away in the forest, here behind the castle."

"Inside the forest, right here?"

"Yes. It was originally a more formal family plot, but it hasn't been used since the eighteen-hundreds, and it wasn't maintained. Most of the burial sites collapsed long ago, and it's now completely overgrown by the forest. The last time I looked, it was just a scattering of fallen stones, all weathered and covered in moss and fir needles. It's now quite impossible to read the headstones, and we can't be sure of who owns what."

David was a little surprised. "I would never have guessed they were all buried here. Is it possible for me to see the graveyard?"

"Certainly – I'd be most happy to show you. But now it's starting to get dark, and I'd have to change into my boots and warm coat. Do you mind if I take you there tomorrow?"

169

"No, of course not. I'll look forward to it very much."

"Yes, so will I. And, you never know, maybe Katarina will join us and reveal which of the gravestones belongs to her." She stepped forward and took his hand affectionately. "Now, I wish to rest for a short while before dinner. I'm a little tired after all this excitement. I hope you've enjoyed discovering more of the castle and finally meeting Katarina. I know that she and the others are very pleased that you've returned."

"Charlotte, I can't thank you enough. I will never forget this afternoon. It's been one of the best moments of my life."

"Excellent. Well, I shall see you in an hour or so, for drinks and dinner. You will bring your wedding chalice, won't you? Remember – the old silver cup I gave you."

"Yes, I have it safe. Tonight will be a great time to use it."

"Very good, David. Now, I know that Hans and Eva have been quite busy in the kitchen. Maybe you would like to join them there. And, please, not a word. They know so little about the castle, and it's better it stays that way."

"Yes, of course. I'll just give them a hand if I can. Hans said he was preparing a *feast*."

"He does tend to exaggerate, though I'm sure we'll eat very well. He's an excellent chef, and very good at desserts too. I particularly like his chocolates."

David laughed. "Yes, they are good. Okay, I'll see you at dinner."

He left her standing in the hallway by her apartment, and went downstairs.

The kitchen resonated with the various sounds of culinary activity – the steaming, bubbling and sizzling of the stove, the random clanking of utensils, and the dull hum of the rangehood. As David entered, he was drenched with the rich aromas of German cooking, and found both Hans and Eva hard at work. While Eva was drying some wine

170

glasses with a handtowel, Hans was at the stove with a half-emptied glass of Weissbier on the bench beside him.

"Hello David!" Eva said, delighted to see him.

Hans turned from the stove. "Hi David. Would you like a beer? I'm having one."

"Hans, I think this is *definitely* time for a Weizen!" David said, starting to feel more at home than ever before.

Hans quickly went to the pantry and came back with a bottle and tall glass. While he poured the beer, Eva was stacking the wine glasses on a shelf.

"So, did you manage to see the Baroness?" she enquired.

"Yes, I've had a great time with her. She told me some of the history of the castle, and showed me more of the antiques in the attic."

"Hmm, that sounds interesting."

Hans handed David a perfectly poured Weizen and grabbed his own glass. "Prost!" he said, and they touched glasses and both took a swig.

"Did she show you her apartment?" Eva asked.

"No, I didn't see that yet."

"She has not let us see it either. We were hoping to get an invitation, but it never comes." Then she whispered, "I start to think there is something secret in there."

David decided not to mention that he would be seeing it the next morning. "Tomorrow, she will show me more of the grounds. I'd like to see the lake; and apparently there's an old cemetery in the forest, just behind the castle."

"Oh, yes!" Hans said, as he placed a tray in the oven. "I saw the cemetery when I was looking for firewood a few weeks ago. That is a creepy place – all the gravestones pushed up and broken by the trees. If there are any ghosts around this castle, that is where they would be."

David gave a small chuckle and took another mouthful of beer. "I should imagine that any self-respecting ghost would prefer to stay in the warmth of the castle, rather than out in the bitter cold of an ancient cemetery."

"I'm sure you are right, but I don't like such places," Eva said, with a shiver. "It's good you have the Baroness to take you there. That place is not for me."

David looked around the kitchen. "I can see you've been busy. Whatever you're doing smells great," he said.

"Yes, I hope so," said Hans. "The Baroness requested that we prepare something special for you, so this is what we are doing. The dinner should be ready in about an hour, and I think I have most things in order. So, let's have a small break and sit in the dining room. We can have another beer while we wait for her."

"Sounds good, but I'll just go to the bedroom for a minute and collect my cup – the one Charlotte gave me. She asked if I could bring it to dinner."

"That's a good idea," said Eva. "And may I take your glass to the dining room?"

"Oh, thankyou – these beers are so big. I'll finish it when I come back."

As he walked down the hallway to the guest room, he started to feel a little tipsy. He'd only had half the Weizen, but it was typically full strength and his tummy was now quite empty. There would be a couple more beers, then the wine at dinner, so he was hoping Hans had some substantial appetizers ready.

He entered the guest room and went straight to his bag in the corner. Just that morning he had wrapped the cup in an old jumper in order to protect it during the trip. Rummaging about for a moment, he found the old jumper, but to his dismay, the cup was not there. He continued to search through the bag. "What the hell?" he whispered to himself. "It *must* be here."

He stood up, questioning how he could have lost it, and gazed vaguely across the room. And there it was – standing neatly on the quilt in the very centre of the bed.

172

"Oh . . . there you are!" he said, deeply amused, and he went to the bed and picked it up.

Suspecting that Katarina may still be there, he looked about, searching for further signs. There was nothing, so he held the cup higher and said, "Thank you. I know what this cup means, and I'll drink to us both. And later tonight, I'll see you again."

It would still be some weeks before Hans and Eva opened their restaurant, but as David entered the dining room, he noticed there were now many more tables and chairs set out evenly across the floor. He joined them at the small table for four, near the fireplace. His beer was waiting for him, and both Hans and Eva had full glasses at the ready. He was also pleased to see a large plate of some sort of vegetable-filled pastry, cut into slices.

"This looks delicious," he said, as he sat down.

"Please, have some," said Hans. "It's a strudel with sauerkraut, but – how do you say? – 'pace yourself', because there is much more to come."

David ate a slice. "Hmm, that's good, thank you." He took a sip of beer and looked about the room. "You seem to be making very good progress with the restaurant."

"Oh, we still have lots more work to do, but you know – slowly, slowly," said Eva.

"Well, I'm sure it will be a great restaurant, and one day I want to return again. In fact, I hope to return many times."

"You will always be welcome," said Hans. "And what about *your* work? I remember you said you were studying."

"Yes – Mechanical Engineering. I still have one year to go, but maybe in the future I could find some work here in Bavaria. I'd need to improve my German, but it's possible."

"Everything is possible," said Eva. "If your heart is there, everything is possible."

They continued to chat and enjoy their pre-dinner drinks, and every now and then Hans would visit the kitchen to briefly check on the food. After half an hour, Charlotte joined them, and they all settled in for an evening of indulgence.

Amidst all the empty chairs and tables spread across the room, theirs was the one table bathed in the glow of candlelight and the radiance of the fire. Throughout the evening, as the other tables remained silent, theirs was vibrant with conversation, laughter, and the sounds of clinking glassware and hearty dining.

They started with a small broth containing chicken, asparagus and thin noodles. Then Hans presented his main course – an entire roasted suckling pig with gold potatoes, mushrooms and cabbage. This was followed by Eva's contribution – a four-layered, rum-infused, thickened cream and chocolate torte, large enough to satisfy a party of ten. And at the end, there was Hans's mandatory selection of superb cheeses and hand-made chocolates.

Somewhere between the suckling pig and the chocolate torte, David finished a rather substantial glass of bock beer, and Charlotte suggested they move to red wine and give a toast. She had two bottles of 1969 Chambolle-Musigny pinot noir sitting to one side, which she had brought specially for the occasion. Hans had been patiently eyeing the bottles for some time, and was delighted to open one and pour for each member of the party. David's special cup was filled as it sat on the table before him, and so too were the other three wine glasses.

Then Charlotte announced, "I wish to propose a toast to you, David, upon your return. You are an excellent young man, and from the very start you have impressed me with your great love of the castle. It has been my pleasure to get to know you better, and to show you even more aspects of our life here. I wish you future happiness." She raised her glass. "To David!" she said, and had a generous mouthful.

"Yes! To David," said Hans, and he took a large draught of the wine.

"To good health and happiness, David," said Eva, before taking a more conservative sip.

"Thank you," he said. "You have all been very kind. I will always remember this most wonderful day." He raised the wedding chalice and drank from it. The wine was smooth and elegant, full of flavour but subtle, as it rolled across his tongue. He continued to hold the cup and studied it closely. Within its silvery curvature, he could see a wide and hazy reflection of the room around him; and for a moment, in that reflection he saw a figure seated in every chair. At every table, they were there – pale, misty, calm and silent – just watching him. He turned his head and looked across the floor. The tables were empty. He focused again on the cup, and the image was gone.

"Are you okay, David?" asked Eva.

"Yes, yes, I'm fine," he said, blinking and returning to the present. "I'd like to propose another toast, if I may." He raised his cup once more. "To good friends, great food and wine, and above all, to the beauty and strength of women, both past and present."

"Well, I'll drink to that!" said Hans, and he took another gulp.

Eva smiled, nodding in agreement, and had another sip.

"That's an excellent toast," said Charlotte. "I couldn't agree more."

Eva stood up from the table. "And with that, I shall go to the kitchen and get the beautiful and strong dessert."

By ten o'clock, they had all taken their fair share of food, drink and conversation, and were thoroughly satisfied. Charlotte wished to retire, and was the first to make a move.

"Thankyou Hans and Eva," she said, getting up slowly. "It has been a lovely dinner, but I'm now quite tired. It's time for me to go upstairs." She glanced at David.

"Yes . . . I think that's enough for me too," he said, feeling a little drunk and sleepy. "Thank you for a great evening, but now I'm going to get a good night's sleep." He made an attempt to pick up some empty plates from the table, but was stopped by Eva.

"Leave them please," she said. "Hans and I will do all these things in the morning."

"Okay, thank you," he said gratefully, and then remembered his cup. "Are you happy to wash my cup, or should I take it now?"

"Oh, I'll take care of the cup," Charlotte said, plucking it up from the table. "Since it's my gift to you, I'd like to clean it. I'll return it to you tomorrow."

"Yes, thank you."

"So, goodnight to you both," said Eva.

"Yes, goodnight. Sleep well," said Hans.

David accompanied Charlotte from the dining room, leaving their hosts sitting at the table, staring quietly into the fire and enjoying the remains of the wine. At the base of the stairs, David stopped and turned to the Baroness. "Well, that was a great dinner," he said. "Goodnight Charlotte. I'll see you tomorrow."

"Yes. You may come to my apartment any time you wish." She held his hand and gave him a small kiss on each cheek. "Sweet dreams, David."

"Yes . . . it's now the time, isn't it? To dream, and to meet Katarina again." He gave her a parting smile, and then made his way slowly down the hallway.

He briefly visited the bathroom, and found himself more tired than ever. In the bedroom, he had just enough strength to kick off his shoes and take off his pants. Then he collapsed into the old bed, pulled up the quilt, and within seconds was sleeping soundly.

It was the heart of the night. A light wind whisked the treetops and swirled across the grounds. The skies had cleared, and the milky glow of a near full moon bathed the castle walls. The moonlight glistened on the frozen lake, and at the edge of the forest, it filtered through the firs and caressed the snow-clad, broken headstones of the cemetery.

Through the window at the end of the hall, it also permeated the gallery, and all the portraits hung sombre and drab in the pallid light.

176

Elsewhere in the castle, the hallways and rooms were still and dark. In their bedroom, Hans and Eva lay fast asleep amid the rhythmic sound of snoring. Around the dining room, the only sounds were a persistent 'tick-tock' from the old clock on the mantle, and a faint crackle from the last embers in the fireplace. In the cold silence of the attic, all the remnants of the past waited lifelessly, and on the upper level, a large pile of cards rested on the small table.

In her apartment, Charlotte sat back in a comfortable armchair and gazed at her painting of the old Gothic church in the field. After some time, she turned to Katarina and her mother, and nodded lightly. Katarina kissed her mother on the forehead and left the room.

Once more, she came to David and lay beside him as he slept. She studied the profile of his face with great affection. "Maximillian," she whispered, then ran her fingers across his forehead and kissed him softly on the lips. Then she closed her eyes and drifted within.

From above, he could see the empty bed move further away. Then the whole room became smaller and smaller until, way below him, it seemed to dissolve behind the castle walls. Still rising, he could see the entire castle sitting within its grounds; then the breadth of the surrounding forest; and finally, the greater hinterland – all saturated by the radiance of the waxing moon. He spun about, facing into the night sky, and was swathed by the shimmering light.

He awoke in clear daylight and felt warm air upon his face. Still feeling a little drowsy, he drew a deep breath and took in the scent of fresh grass and the sweet fragrance of flowers. The chirping of small birds and the hum of insects filled the air. As he sat up, he found he had been sleeping in the shade of a large oak tree, and the wide, open fields around him were immersed in the full sunshine of late spring. A handsome, black horse was grazing a short distance away. Its mane was long; its smooth coat gleaming in the strong light. Beyond, in the middle distance, stood a beautiful and solitary stone church. There was not a person in sight.

177

He got up slowly, brushed himself off, and walked over to the horse. Taking hold of the reins, he gave it a couple of firm pats on the neck and looked it in the eye. It turned its head toward him, gave a short, deep neigh, and didn't flinch. This horse knew him well.

Riding towards the church, he felt the powerful rhythm of its canter and the bright sun warming his back. She would be there, he thought. Perhaps, they were all there. He went inside, but as his eyes adjusted to the dim light, he discovered it was empty. Just the cool air, and the earthy smells of hewn hardwood and stone.

He rode once around the church and failed to find her. Then he scanned the open fields, all the way to the rim of the distant forest. It was the strong contrast between the darkness of the forest and the brilliance of her pure-white horse that immediately caught his eye. The horse stood there, motionless – the faint outline of its rider, just visible.

At a gallop, the rich green field moved swiftly beneath him, and before long, he was approaching the edge of the forest. As he neared, he could see her dismount and stand there waiting – her long, dark hair falling about the shoulders and sides of a slender crimson robe. Then, pulling up, he was struck once again by the sheer beauty of her face and the tenderness of her smile. She held out her hand to him, and he got down from his horse and left it breathing heavily from the sprint. He took her in his arms and they embraced each other tightly.

"You have returned," she said softly, with her head resting on his shoulder.

He cradled her face in his hands and gazed into her gentle, blue eyes.

"I waited a long time," she said.

"Yes, I know . . . but you'll wait no longer." He kissed her passionately.

Then, leaving the horses to graze, she took him by the hand and led him into the forest.

178

Eva woke much later than usual, but it was Sunday and she didn't mind. She had a shower and got dressed. Then she left Hans fast asleep in the room and went downstairs. Every floor was quiet, and she was happy to attend to some tasks while the others slept in.

After an hour, she had stoked and relit the main fireplace, cleared the dining table and got the kitchen back in order. It was now late morning and the time for breakfast had come and gone. Hans staggered into the kitchen wearing his dressing gown and poured himself a large glass of water from the tap. Eva took one look at him and made some strong coffee. Then they sat down and started to chat about the previous day.

By midday, Hans had also got himself showered and dressed, and returned downstairs. They still hadn't seen or heard from David, and began to wonder whether he could still be sleeping. They speculated that he may have already woken and gone directly to visit Charlotte. They thought it was strange though, that coming from the guest room, he would not stop and greet them first. He would have to pass right by. Surely, he must still be sleeping.

Eva always liked to have a clear view of the day ahead, and now she was wondering whether her guest would be joining them for lunch. And since he had made plans to see the grounds with Charlotte, if he was still in his room, she may also be waiting. So, Eva thought it was probably wisest to check on him.

Leaving Hans in the kitchen, she went down the hall and found the guestroom door closed. She listened carefully for a moment, with her ear pressed against the door, but heard nothing. She gave a couple of small knocks and listened again. "David, are you there?" she asked through the door. There was no response.

Very carefully, she opened the door a little and peeked inside the softly-lit room. The air was unusually cool. Looking over to the bed, she could see the contour of his body under the quilt, and his head resting peacefully on the pillow. He was asleep.

"David, I'm sorry to wake you, but the time is . . ." She stopped. Something was wrong. Hesitantly, she stepped into the room and gazed at him. "Ahh! David!" she cried in shock, holding her hands to her chest.

His eyes were closed, and his face as pale as the snow. His lips were ashen. There was not the slightest movement of the quilt upon his chest. Not a single breath passed. Just a silent and grim serenity.

Distraught, Eva ran from the room and down the hall, calling to Hans. He was greatly distressed by the news, and almost in disbelief, he returned with Eva to the guestroom. He placed his hand on David's forehead and confirmed that he was cold.

Even though it seemed he had passed away during the night, Eva was filled with regret that she hadn't come to check on him earlier. Having become so fond of their guest, a deep sorrow descended on the couple, and they stood there in contemplation for some time. "What could have happened?" they asked themselves. He looked so peaceful. It was disturbing and inexplicable, but they also agreed that they knew so little about him.

They went straight upstairs to the Baroness's apartment and knocked firmly on the main door. After several seconds there was no answer, so they knocked again. "Charlotte!" they called. There was still no response, so they tried the door. It was locked securely. They looked at each other with a degree of fear. Surely, she hasn't also come to harm, they thought. But she's not answering, and why is the door locked? The idea that something may have happened to her, scared them. But then, Eva thought they shouldn't be alarmed quite yet. Perhaps Charlotte is simply not in her apartment.

She strode down the hallway and stopped at the stairwell. There was a chance the Baroness had gone upstairs to the attic, but it was unlikely. Eva pondered for a second, then went to the end of the hall and looked out the main window. It was a glorious, sunny day, and she had a clear view across the castle forecourt, and all the way to the frozen lake and the edge of the forest.

"Hans, komm her!" she called out, and he hurried over and stood beside her.

In the distance, by the side of the lake, they could see Charlotte dressed in full winter attire. She seemed to be enjoying the fresh air and sunshine, as she casually strolled through the snow-laden grounds.

Part 5 – Epilogue

The death of the young Australian was kept out of the news. Charlotte did not desire any form of publicity regarding such an unfortunate event. Nor did Hans and Eva. Contact was made with the local Police Commander, whom Charlotte had known for many years, and the case was assigned directly to a detective from Munich.

By mid-afternoon, both the detective and a forensics officer arrived at the castle in a large, unmarked van. They made an initial examination of David's body and the guestroom, and were then guided by Charlotte through the various other parts of the castle he had visited. They could find nothing of importance to the investigation in either the dining room, hallways, gallery or stairwell. Also, they could see nothing of relevance in the attic; although, due to the intense cold and fading light, their time there was brief.

While accompanying the officers, Charlotte explained how she had befriended the young tourist who had taken a great interest in the castle, and had told her he would love to return. A question was raised as to why she had paid for his flight to Munich. She said that since David was a student and a person of good character, she was very pleased to assist him. Like Hans and Eva, she said she did not know him very well, and had no idea whether he had any medical history. Hans said they had all eaten the same food, and drank the same wine, and he invited a thorough inspection of the kitchen. They all agreed that their guest had enjoyed his time at the castle, and were now deeply saddened and could not account for the death.

By the evening, formal statements had been taken, and the scene photographed. David's body and possessions were then removed and taken to Munich for a complete examination. The results of the post mortem were inconclusive. They could find no physical cause. The pathology report revealed no sign of infection, no apparent toxins, and although there was some alcohol in his system, it was not enough to be significant. A study of his clothing and other personal items was unremarkable, but the analysis of his camera did reveal two rather striking photographs taken in the vicinity. One was of the castle itself, as seen from the lake's edge; and the other was of a local church.

After further investigation, Jason was located by the police in London, and informed of his friend's death. Later, the detective was able to interview him by telephone. Deeply depressed by the news, Jason confirmed that his companion had liked his stay at the castle, but could not understand why he had returned. When Jason started to speak of ghosts and scary portraits, the detective decided that his credibility was questionable.

David's father was contacted by police in Sydney, and in a state of shock he immediately travelled to Munich. He could provide no explanation for the death of his son, saying he was a good sportsman and had been in the peak of health. He made a brief visit to the castle, wishing to retrace David's final moments and speak to the people who had last seen him alive. It was a solemn affair, but Charlotte, Hans and Eva all convinced him that David had been immensely happy there. They invited his father to stay, but he declined and returned to Munich.

The finding of the Coroner was that the exact cause of death could not be determined. The report speculated that it was perhaps some rare and inexplicable aberration of the heart. The detective was not happy with the result, sensing that something unusual must have occurred in the castle, but he had no other avenues to pursue.

The authorities released David's body and allowed his burial. With a heavy heart, his father considered whether he would bury him in Munich, recognising that for many years his son had spoken of his love of Bavaria, and his great desire to travel there. Finally, though, after thinking long and hard on the matter, he decided to return David's body to Sydney, where he would be buried beside his mother.

From all parts of the region, they came. From every generation – men, women, and children. Many knew him well. Many had only heard the story. Of how a knight had failed to return, and how his wife had waited. They came from their favourite places – from their places of comfort and rest. From the castles, taverns, old dwellings and ruins. From the churches, belltowers, halls and village squares. From the forests, lakes, barns and graveyards. They all came to welcome him, and to praise Katarina for her patience.

The castle forecourt was crowded, and as Maximillian moved among them, he was warmly greeted by all. He made his way to the front door and was embraced by a close comrade from his first campaign. As he proceeded through the main hall and up the stairway, the long lines applauded as he passed. He entered the gallery on the first floor, where the family had assembled, and they gave welcoming smiles and slowly parted as he continued to the end of the hall. There, Katarina and Charlotte were waiting. Next to them, on the wall, were two portraits, side by side. Below them, on the hallstand, the crystal vase had been removed, and in its place rested the beautiful, silver cup.

* * * * * * * * * * * * *

Made in the USA
Monee, IL
01 November 2020